# RIDE AGAINST THE WIND

## Also by Terrell L. Bowers

*The Secret of Snake Canyon*

# RIDE AGAINST THE WIND

## Terrell L. Bowers

Walker and Company
New York

First published in the United States of America in 1996 by Walker Publishing Company, Inc.

Published simultaneously in Canada by Thomas Allen & Son Canada, Limited, Markham, Ontario

Library of Congress Cataloging-in-Publication Data
Bowers, Terrell L.
Ride against the wind / Terrell L. Bowers.
p. cm.
ISBN 0-8027-4156-8
I. Title.
PS3552.O87324R5   1996
813'.54—dc20      96-18656
CIP

Printed in the United States of America

2  4  6  8  10  9  7  5  3  1

*For Patricia, my wife, lover, and best friend.*

# RIDE AGAINST THE WIND

# CHAPTER 1

PAUSING TO BRUSH a damp lock of auburn hair from her forehead, eighteen-year-old Marian Gates leaned against the heavily laden wagon to catch her breath. Daylight was on the wane, but the partially exposed sun and the humidity from the three-day rainstorm caused the earth to swelter. Her hair clung to her moist brow, and her shoulders and upper body were damp from perspiration. Trying to get her team and wagon out of the mire was exhausting work.

She slogged through the mud, sinking in over her ankles. For the dozenth time, she took up the loose ends of the reins and swatted the team on the rumps. "Git!" she cried. "Come on, you boneheads! Pull!"

The two horses responded halfheartedly, surging against the traces, digging into the soft ground. Marian grabbed hold of the spokes and used her every ounce of strength, attempting to force the front wheel to turn. However, the wagon was buried to the hubs and the entire effort, both by Marian and the horses, barely caused the heavy wagon to rock.

"Damn!" Using profanity was rare for Marian, but she was completely frustrated. "We'll never get out!"

The horses ceased their straining and she let go of the wheel. It was growing late and all of her efforts had been wasted. She had forced branches and sagebrush into the muck in front of the wheels, but they were embedded too deeply. She took a step back into a hole and sank to her knee in the oozing muck.

She sought a firm footing with her other foot and strug-

1

gled to pull free. She was successful—in part. Her foot slipped out of the mud, and her shoe at the same time.

"Oh, for the love of—!" Teetering on one leg, she reached into the bog, took hold of her shoe, and pulled. The suction was tremendous. She rocked her weight back and applied all her energy to the chore. The shoe gave a little, then dislodged suddenly, causing her to land seat-first in the mud!

Tears of defeat burned her eyes, as she was instantly assailed by the cold liquid seeping through her clothes. The wagon was out of reach, so she had to rotate her body and bury her hands in the slime to gain enough leverage to get her knees under her. The heavy skirt and petticoats were pinned down by weight, preventing her from standing back up. In a fit of exasperation, Marian forgot everything but ridding herself of the clinging morass. She pitched forward onto her hands and knees, then battled up to her feet. She lifted her skirt out of the slop and waded to the bank. When she reached shore, she collapsed on the damp ground.

Lying on her back, she closed her eyes and drew in great gulps of air. She could feel the mud that was caked to her clothes, arms, and legs beginning to dry.

Perhaps I'll die right here, she thought morbidly. Her present condition would save anyone the chore of burying her because she was covered with so much muck already.

"Well, take a gander off yonder, Bingo," a sneering voice shattered the afternoon stillness. "Looks to be some sort of creature over there that has crawled out of the creek bed."

Marian jumped, her eyes popping open. She sat up quickly and saw Jerrod Danmyer on horseback, on the other side of the stream, not thirty feet away.

"How dare you spy on me, Danmyer!" she said, her voice shrill.

Jerrod leaned back in the saddle, astride a magnificent black mare. He chuckled as he directed his words to his horse. "Durned if that mud creature don't sound human, Bingo. You suppose it's some kind of mermaid?" He pursed his lips and gave a negative shake of his head. "Nope, that ain't it."

"Are you quite through making fun at my expense?"

"I've got it!" he said, continuing to tease her. "I'll bet it's some kind of mud cat that usually spawns in the Arkansas River. Now it's come down Raccoon Creek and got itself landlocked."

Marian took a moment to pull the hem of her skirt down about her ankles. She wiped at a fleck of mud on her cheek but made it a wide smear. Ignoring the man as best she could, she shook some of the loose muck from her hands.

"Only the lowest scum on earth," she replied, "would laugh at someone else's distress. It's plain that Stover was right about you Danmyers—there isn't a gentleman in the whole family."

"Your pa has us pegged there. 'Course, I ain't real sure that there's a lady under all that mud you're packing, either."

"Go away and leave me alone!"

"Not till I figure out what you're doing."

"What am I doing?" she snapped. "I'm trying to learn to swim, so I thought I'd start out in a puddle and work my way up to a pond!"

He chuckled again—this time at her cynical humor. As he dismounted, he dropped the reins and his mare stood obediently immobile. Without looking in her direction, Jerrod walked to the edge of the mire and studied the marooned wagon.

It had been a good many months since Marian had last seen Jerrod. She was unsure of his exact age, but guessed him to be in his late twenties. He had a wiry build and his mahogany-brown hair showed from under his flat-crowned hat. His face was lean and his eyes a stormy grayish-blue. The way he moved reminded her of a timber wolf, one that had staved off famine long enough to reach maturity.

He turned toward her and said, "Appears you got in belly-deep before you stopped the team, mud kitten. Reckon you know that this shortcut is used mostly by riders on horseback."

Clumsily rising to her feet, she squared her shoulders and met his smirk boldly.

"I thought my team could pull through the bog. It appeared firm enough, until I'd committed the wagon. Besides that, I came across this very spot this morning."

"This morning was cool, so the ground was more solid," he said matter-of-factly. "And I imagine the wagon was empty, rather than packing a full load of wood."

Marian swallowed her pride, for he was absolutely right. She had been in a hurry to get home and had risked the soggy crossing. Now she was hopelessly stuck. In a voice that was uncharacteristically meek and childlike, she asked, "Can you help me get out?"

"You're not asking a lowly Danmyer to actually help you? What would your pa say about that?"

"Stover will likely take a strap to me for being so late. I'm supposed to be home by dark!"

Jerrod lifted his eyes skyward and grunted. "Unless you've got a pair of wings, you ain't going to make it before nightfall. It's a good ten miles to your house, and that sun is sinking pretty fast."

Marian shielded her eyes and checked the sun's position. There was not more than an hour of daylight left. Even if she could start the team moving right now, it would be impossible to reach home before dusk. She cringed, thinking of Stover's flash-fire temper. More than that, of the leather strap he kept hanging on the wall of the woodshed.

"Please, Mr. Danmyer, I'm asking for your help."

He tipped back his flat-crowned hat with a single slender finger and stared at her in wonder. "*Mister* Danmyer?" he repeated. "You must be getting desperate, calling me Mister."

"Are you going to help or not!"

"I'll see what I can do."

Jerrod studied the team and wagon for a few long seconds. Then he hooked a thumb upstream. "There's a pool at the bend where you can wash some of that mud off." As she looked in that direction, he went to his horse and swung aboard. Crossing to her side of the stream, he reached into his saddlebags and withdrew a towel.

"Here," he said, tossing her the cloth.

Marian took the towel and hurried along the bank, carrying one dirty shoe. She hoped that Jerrod was not watching her, for she certainly had an ungainly gait wearing only one shoe.

The creek was about twenty feet across and ran from a foot deep to double that in places. Someone had once told her that Raccoon Creek wound across Kansas until it joined the Arkansas River somewhere. She didn't know about that, but she did know the water was usually cold.

When she reached the edge of the creek, Marian glanced back over her shoulder. A bend in the trail allowed her to move out of Jerrod's sight. She placed the clean towel on a grassy patch and waded into the middle of the stream. She splashed water onto her skirt and worked the material between her fingers, trying to remove the caked mud and clean the soiled spots. Fearful of her father's wrath should the dress be ruined, she went to the deepest part of the pool and sat right down.

The icy chill of the water penetrated her clothes at once. Marian sucked in her breath, as the level of the cold stream hit her well above the waist. She exhaled in short gasps, shivering violently, as she splashed water up into her face and hurried to scrub her clothes and bathe at the same time.

After a few minutes, she decided that there was no need

for half measures. She ducked her head until she could wash the dirt out of her hair. The freezing water ran down her neck and appended bumps on her already raised gooseflesh. She shuddered violently from the cold, but was determined to rid herself of the mud.

"What in blazes are you doing, lady?" Jerrod's harsh words burst into her privacy. "Are you plumb loco?"

Marian blinked at the water in her eyes. Before she could manage a reply, Jerrod had waded out to her. He grabbed hold of her arm and gave a yank. She scrambled to get her footing, as he practically dragged her out of the creek.

"I—I was . . ." She trembled, clenching her teeth to keep them from chattering. "I just wanted to get—"

"Pneumonia, you crazy sodbuster! You'll catch your death! I thought you'd dry yourself off, not take a bath! Talk about doing something stupid."

"I am not stupid!" She defended herself vehemently. "Don't call me stupid!"

"Even the smartest people sometimes make stupid choices," he countered, "and what you just did was plain stupid."

She might have debated the point, but he took hold of her wrist once more and led her back to where her wagon was stuck. He stopped next to his horse, released his grip on her, and reached up to untie his bedroll. She displayed a confused look when he shoved a blanket into her arms.

"Go behind the brush and get those wet duds off. I'll round up some dry tinder for a fire."

Marian stared inanely at the blanket. "You can't seriously expect me to . . . to disrobe?"

"Get a move on!" He fired the words at her. "I'll be hanged if I take the blame for your dying from a chill."

She backed away, fearful that Jerrod might decide to help her undress. Once behind the bushes, she began to work the fasteners loose on her bodice. Trying to sew up a flour sack with a pitchfork would have been a simple task compared to shedding her clothing.

"Where you at, farmer girl?" Jerrod called out. "Time is a-wasting!"

Marian wrapped herself securely in the blanket and gathered up her wet clothes.

"You need some help?" he asked.

"I'm coming!" she retorted sharply, picking her way carefully through the brush. "Did you ever try and walk barefoot through this stuff?"

Her show of temper appeared to cool Jerrod's ire. As she came into sight, he nodded toward a campfire.

"I've strung a rope for your things. You warm yourself while I hang your clothes to dry."

"We don't have time for this," she complained. "Stover is going to come looking for me."

"It won't take any longer to dry your clothes than it will for me to get your wagon unstuck."

Marian felt a spark of hope. "Then you can get it out?"

Jerrod did not answer for a time. He had built his fire between three saplings and formed a semicircle clothesline by looping his rope to each one and back. He took the bundle from her and draped her skirt over the rope, nearest the flames, then her bodice. The other garments were then spread to either side, with her shoes placed on the ground a couple of feet from the fire pit.

Marian padded over to the side of the fire and put a hand out to warm her chilled fingers. Simultaneously, she felt the heat against her face, both from inside as well as out. She had never been so self-conscious in her life.

"You can sit down on the poncho. Keep adding wood to the fire."

Marian had not noticed the oilskin slicker that he'd spread out on the ground next to a pile of branches. She knelt onto it and curled her legs under her until she was sitting down.

"I don't suppose you brought any grub with you, mud kitten?"

"N-no. I expected to be home by this time."

"Just you and the load of wood, huh?"

"We need a new fence to keep our cow and team in at nights. The posts are for building a corral."

He snorted. "Then you haven't eaten since breakfast." It was a statement. "Ever think that you might get caught in another storm, that you might have a breakdown on the trail, end up with a lame horse?"

She sorely wished she had encountered Jerrod under different circumstances. She would have enjoyed telling the haughty, self-righteous Danmyer to go kiss a chicken on the lips. However, what possible ammunition could she muster to counter him in this situation?

"How did you happen by?" she said, changing the subject. "Were you on your way into town?"

He cocked his head toward his saddle and gear. A long, skinny pole was strapped along the rifle sheath. "I took the afternoon off to do some fishing. There're several pools— like the one where you decided to take a bath—that are good fishing holes. I caught enough for supper, but it looks as if we'll be eating them right here."

"Really, Mr. Danmyer, I don't want to eat your fish. I must get home. Stover—"

"Yeah, I know all about your father."

"Can you get the wagon out?"

"It's going to take some time. I'll have to unload the posts first. If lightening the wagon still doesn't allow the horses to go forward, we'll have to unhitch them and try and pull the wagon out the way it went in. Either way, it's going to take a couple hours."

Marian looked about nervously. "A couple of hours?"

"If we can get it out at all," he replied. "We might have to wait until it gets cold enough to firm up the ground. That would be closer to daylight."

"No!" she said a bit too emphatically. Recovering at once, she softened her voice. "I mean, I have to get home. Stover has a . . ." She didn't want to mention the strap or his temper. "He'll worry about me."

"We'll have something to eat and dry out your things as best we can. Then I'll unload the wagon. Bingo ought to be able to help the team back the wagon up a little. If we can get a run at it, your horses might have enough momentum to start the wagon moving forward. Once they get going, they should be able to pull out of the bog."

"Then we'll have to reload the posts?"

"Right."

She sighed deeply. His logic and her stuck wagon seemed to offer no alternative. "All right, Mr. Danmyer. I would love to share your fish."

# CHAPTER 2

THERE WAS A strained silence between Marian and Jerrod during the meal. He had fixings in his saddlebags because he frequently ate on the trail. He used a handful of flour and a little salt on the fish. He also had a tin of beans, which he warmed next to a small pot of coffee.

Marian ate quietly, graciously accepting the two fish he prepared for her and a portion of the beans. He had only a single cup for the coffee, which he gave to her. He himself drank from the pot. When they finished the meager feast, he opened another tin. To her surprise, it was an airtight of peaches.

She refrained from mentioning that she and her family had not enjoyed the luxury of canned fruit in over two years. He took only a couple of bites and then handed the container to her. She savored every morsel, even drinking the juice to empty the container. To her chagrin, the action did not pass unnoticed.

"Hate to waste the syrup," she said self-consciously.

"Been a dry spell for the Gates family, I suppose. Taters and beans are likely your steady diet."

"We have corn and other vegetables too. We're no more impoverished than most of the other farmers."

He raised his brows. "Impoverished?"

"A polite word I learned in a book." She waited for his reaction. "Mrs. Loring taught a good many of us how to read. Max has several books that he passes around for anyone who wants to read."

"Max Loring is a good man."

"I don't recall ever seeing you at his Sunday meetings."

10

"I'm sure you know that we Danmyers aren't exactly welcome at those meetings."

"You shouldn't think that."

"Weather's been fair for a couple seasons," he said, changing the subject. "And the crops look good for you farmers this year."

"What about you, Mr. Danmyer? Has your family always been rich and powerful?"

He stared into the fire, the flickering light reflecting in his eyes.

"My pa and his brother settled in this part of the country years before the first German immigrants arrived—or you Ohio farmers either. My uncle was killed while fighting in one of the half-dozen Indian wars. Pa has battled month-long blizzards in the winter and year-long droughts in the summer. Because of the hardships he endured, Pa selected the best possible land and built our home. I suppose some folks think that makes us greedy."

Marian felt ashamed for the question. "I sometimes forget that your family were the first settlers here."

"The town was named Eden, in honor of my mother. Her name was Eve."

"Stover claims all of you Danmyers are evil."

"Your father is entitled to his opinion, but we Danmyers never start trouble. If we end up in a fight, you can bet someone else started it."

"Like at the Christmas festival?"

"I only asked a girl to dance. I wasn't the one who started the fight."

"I noticed that your brother and hired hands were quick to jump in and start swinging."

"Maybe you also noticed I was slightly overmatched, with a half-dozen farmers pounding on me. If Vince and the Sanchez boys hadn't entered into the foray, I might have been killed. That's why we no longer attend any of your Sunday meetings."

"You're saying it's not your fault."

"That's right. We Danmyers don't go looking for trouble."

"What about the treachery done by your brother, Faron Danmyer? He kidnapped my uncle Zeb's betrothed, Laura Bonnet. When Uncle Zeb tried to get her back, Faron killed him!"

"And then Faron forced her to marry him, huh?" He grunted. "Now, that don't sound far-fetched, does it?"

"What do you mean?"

"You tell a fancy story," he said, "but I expect the only truth about it is the fact that Faron was forced to defend himself and did kill Zeb Gates."

"Do you deny that he stole Laura from our family, a woman who traveled with us all the way from Ohio, and who was Zeb's intended bride?"

"I was off fighting in the war at the time, but I can tell you, there was no kidnapping involved. Faron and Laura met and fell in love."

*"What?"* She was incredulous. "That's ridiculous!"

"Laura told Zeb that she couldn't marry him, that she was in love with another man. Zeb wouldn't accept that. He came after Faron with a gun and tried to kill him. Faron was a better shot than your uncle."

"You're lying!"

A darkness entered Jerrod's face, a warning that she had overstepped the bounds of civil conversation. "I better get that wagon unloaded or the next thing I know, I'll be getting myself accused of kidnapping *you!*"

Jerrod swung up onto the mare and rode it over to her wagon. He stepped from the stirrup onto the wagon and began to toss the posts in the direction of the shore.

She decided to rinse off the frying pan, tins, and pot used for the meal. Trying to keep the blanket securely about her at the same time was more than a little awkward.

Jerrod finished unloading the wagon, then forced the

team to back up a step or two. After managing that, he rose to his feet, slapped the reins on the animal's rumps, and shouted, "*Ye-hah!*"

The team jumped ahead in surprise. The wagon started forward, until it entered the hole. There it lodged for a split second, then came free. The powerful horses pulled and bucked against the soggy mire until they were out onto the firm bank. The wagon followed, rolling onto solid ground.

"You did it!" Marian shouted happily. "You did it!"

Jerrod set the brake and climbed down. He took a moment to stroke and speak gently to each horse. When he came back to the fire, Marian could not hide her jubilation.

"I—I don't know how to thank you," she said, smiling for the first time. "I would have been stuck all night."

Jerrod met her eyes. For a moment he seemed to share her happiness, but when he spoke, his voice was void of emotion. "Still have to reload the wagon."

"I will get dressed and help with that."

He stepped over to check the condition of her clothes. He simpered playfully as he purposely chose her underdress for his test. "Your dainties ain't even dry yet. Be at least another hour."

Hiding her mortification, she replied, "I'll wear them damp. I must get home as soon as possible."

"You stick by the fire while I load the wagon," he told her. "The temperature's sinking like a rock in a puddle and there's no point in your having on those cold, damp clothes any longer than necessary."

Marian agreed. All she could do was wait until the wagon was loaded and her clothes were dry. In the meantime, she prayed Stover didn't show up. If he were to catch her in such a compromising situation, there would be no words to stop his wrath. He would undoubtedly try to kill Jerrod without waiting for an explanation.

"Soon as I finish loading, we'll get started."

"We?"

"Never know when a party of Cheyenne or Sioux Indians will come riding though. We've been fortunate to avoid any major attacks, but there has been some stolen cattle and a few sightings. I think even your pa would agree that being caught alone by several warriors would be worse than being in my company."

"I wouldn't wager money on that bet."

Jerrod ignored the remark and walked over to the stack of posts. Adroitly, he began to load them back into the wagon. The chore took him the better part of thirty minutes.

As he neared the end, Marian grabbed her clothes and moved behind the brush once more. The garments were still damp, but she jerked on the clothes anyway, except for the muddy shoes. They were beyond help and so stiff she could not have gotten her feet into them.

At her return, she discovered Jerrod's horse tied to the back of the wagon. Jerrod was kicking dirt over the smoldering embers of the fire.

She paused to roll up the blanket she had been wearing and pick up the poncho. Remembering that it was usual to wrap the slicker outside the blanket, she spread it out and began to put it back the same way.

Jerrod put away the tin plates and frying pan. When she carried the blanket roll over, he tied it behind his saddle.

"You don't need to see me home, Mr. Danmyer. I'll be all right."

"It's no trouble, mud kitten."

She grimaced. "Would you stop calling me that? I don't find it very flattering."

"Well, if you take pause to think back, ma'am, you may recall that you never have introduced yourself to me."

"You know who I am!"

"Only that you are a member of the Gates family."

"I've seen you around for the ten years we have lived in Eden. We practically grew up together."

"Did we?"

"And I've seen you looking my way more than once. Don't tell me you don't know my name."

"That's rather assuming," he replied. "Why should I care who you are?"

"I think you do . . . because of the way you have looked at me before."

"The way I looked at you?"

"How many eligible girls are there in Eden, Mr. Danmyer?"

"Between the ages of fourteen and twenty-three? Sixteen, not counting one widow."

"And I'll bet you can name each and every one."

He grinned. "Your argument is a good one, Miss Gates. I reckon I have taken a gander at you on occasion."

"Then can we drop the 'mud kitten' name? I feel dirty enough without that reminder."

"On one condition."

"And that is?"

"That we set aside our differences and pretend to be friends. You can call me by my first name, and I'll do the same for you."

"No. We couldn't do that."

"Why not?"

"Stover would kill both of us, if he ever found out. You don't know him."

"I know you call him Stover instead of Pa or Father."

"It is out of respect. Even my mother calls him Mr. Gates."

"I guess most fathers are like that. My own insisted that I call him sir until I reached the age of twenty-one."

"And what do you call him now?"

Jerrod again showed humor. "Usually sir."

"Then you must understand why we can't be on a first-name basis."

"Sorry, I guess I'll keep calling you mud kitten."

"We don't have time for this foolishness. I must get home!"

"I'm not holding you up. Just call me by my first name and we'll be kicking up trail dust."

"All right!" she snapped vehemently. "Can we go now, . . . Jerrod?"

The victory in his eyes was not in his voice. In fact, he spoke to her with a mellow offering that was smooth as silk. "Climb aboard, Marian. Hate to wait for Stover to come looking for you."

They rode in silence for the next hour. Marian was uncomfortable, but her clothes had dried to the point where she was no longer cold. She tried to rehearse what she would say to Stover, but her mind would not cooperate. All she could think about was the man at her side.

Could he have been telling the truth about Zeb Gates? Had he gone off in a jealous rage and forced Faron Danmyer to kill him in self-defense? The story was a far cry from the way it had been told to her.

"I was quite young when we moved to Eden," she began softly. "I hardly remember Laura Bonnet. I know she was fairly attractive and had a wonderfully musical voice. I still have an impression of her singing at Sunday meetings."

"I didn't meet her till after she was my sister-in-law," Jerrod replied. "I went off to fight in the War between the States on my sixteenth birthday. Faron was already married upon my return."

"So you have only hearsay as to the story?"

"My father told me about it. Faron and Laura had already moved to Colorado. Faron got himself a small ranch. They have a couple kids now."

"Laura traveled with our wagon train. She was promised to Zeb."

"Life don't always follow a straight line, Marian. Pa told me that Faron met her by accident and he loved her from that moment on. They didn't mean to fall in love, it just happened. You don't know my oldest brother. He was not a fighter or troublemaker. Why do you suppose that I went to fight in the war instead of him? After all, he was eight years older than me."

"He refused to fight in the war?"

"Faron was strong, able, and a passable shot, but he didn't want to hurt anyone. Even as a kid, it was Vince and I who had to shoot the rabbits for supper or go on the hunting trips for deer. Faron even hated the chore of branding our own cattle, because he knew it caused the animals pain. His heart was about as soft as that bog you were in."

"Stover blames your family, not just Faron."

"Yeah, I know."

"It would be best for you not to go all the way into our yard. I'll tell Stover that I got stuck and that's all."

"You would lie to your own father?"

She felt a pang of guilt. "I . . . I would not lie to him, only omit certain events. He is a very caring man. I don't doubt for a minute that he would lay down his life for my mother or any of us kids. But he is also a very strict man who deplores weakness or excuses."

"Well, we have nothing to hide from him. Any good neighbor would have stuck around and helped you out of that mire. I don't intend to sneak around behind the man's back."

Marian took her bearings and located a familiar field of corn to one side of the trail. Oddly enough, she was saddened that the journey was close to an end.

"Looks as if your old man wasn't all that concerned about you. I don't see any search parties."

"By this hour, he must have assumed that I stayed over at the Krugers'. They are our closest friends and live quite close to the main road."

The wagon rocked and creaked as it entered the yard. Jerrod rolled up to the front of the sod house and stopped. He set the brake and jumped down from the box.

Marian started after him, then hesitated, surprised that he turned and reached up for her. She found the step with her bare foot, then his hands went about her waist and lowered her to the ground.

"What'n thunder is going on!" a grating voice bellowed from the doorway. "Marian! Is that you?"

"Yes, sir," she answered, reaching up to snatch hold of her shoes and quickly stepping away from Jerrod. She hurried around to the opposite side of the wagon to confront Stover.

"Do you know the hour, gal?" Stover demanded a reply. "I've told you a thousand times not to be riding after dark!"

Jerrod followed after her. His own voice was sarcastic. "Maybe you ought to concern yourself that the young lady is all right."

"Who be there in the dark?" he growled, squinting against the darkness.

"I got stuck at the creek crossing," Marian hurried to reply. "This man was kind enough to help me get out and see me home safely."

Recognition entered Stover's face. "Danmyer!" He made the name sound dirty. "If you touched my girl, I'll rip you apart like a rag doll!"

Jerrod displayed a cocky grin. "Don't get all mushy with gratitude, Gates. If it had been you in the mud, I'd have left you for the buzzards."

"Get off my property, Danmyer! You ain't welcome here!"

Marian placed herself between the two men, fearful that they would start to fight. Stover was hard as steel, unbending, dogmatic, and poised to kill. She risked a swift backhand but stood in his way.

"I would have had to spend night there, sir, if Mr. Danmyer had not come along. We owe him a debt of thanks."

"Take a body no more than three hours to walk here from the slough crossing," he retorted. "You could have—" He stopped short, taking note of her soiled clothing. When he spied her bare feet, fury reddened his face.

She quickly explained. "I spent an hour slopping about in the mud, trying to get out, sir. By the time I realized I was hopelessly stuck, I could never have reached home before dark."

Stover reached out and shoved her to one side. He wore only his pants and boots over his long-handles, but he was ready to wade in and fight with Jerrod.

"You got about two seconds to get off of our property, Danmyer," he hissed. "If you ain't gone by then, I'm going to whoop you to the point of death and tie you over your horse, belly first!"

Jerrod was about the same six-foot height as Stover, both of them big men. Marian's father had more weight, but each man was lean and hard. The two of them exchanged icy stares, but Jerrod did not push back.

"Always a pleasure to help out a neighbor," he said thickly. "I reckon I'll be going."

"We did nothing wrong, sir," Marian maintained quietly. "Mr. Danmyer was only being considerate in seeing me home safely."

"Ain't nothing considerate about a Danmyer." Stover grated the words.

Jerrod went to the back of the wagon, untied Bingo, and swung up into the saddle lightly. To Marian's dismay, he paused to tip his hat to her.

"I'll say good-night to you, mud kitten." He flashed a

cocky grin at Stover and held up a hand of farewell. "And a good-night to you too, Mr. Gates."

Marian watched him ride away, and within moments he was lost to the darkness of the moonless night.

Wilma Gates had donned a robe and come to the door. She shook her head at the sight of Marian standing there in soiled clothes, shoes in one hand, hair as tangled as if she had tried to brush it with a handful of cockleburs.

"Dear girl, you look as if you were dragged through a pen of wildcats. What on earth happened?"

"Go back to bed, Wilma," Stover ordered her gently. "You can speak to Marian in the morning."

"Yes, Mr. Gates," was her mother's subservient reply. Then she was quickly back into the house.

Marian was given no such relief. Stover's callused hand locked about her wrist and he pulled her away from the house a few steps. Once out of earshot, he stopped and jerked her about to face him.

"Let me hear it, gal." His voice was deep and threatening. "Tell me exactly what took place."

Marian swallowed against her pounding heart. During her life, she had suffered a number of trips to the woodshed for punishment. She recognized the menace in his face. With the combination of worry over her arriving late and then discovering that she had been with a hated Danmyer, he was worked to a furor. If she chose the wrong words, she would end up feeling a strap over her bare back.

"It is exactly as I told you, sir. The wagon bogged down at the Raccoon Creek crossing. I tried everything to get out, but the wagon was in too deep. When Mr. Danmyer arrived, I had removed my shoes to try and clean off some of the mud."

His gaze burned into her, searching for any shred of deceit. The shadows helped Marian to hide some of the apprehension she was experiencing. There was no wind in her lungs and her heart seemed to have stopped beating.

"You knew he was a Danmyer, yet you rode home with him."

"He refused to let me make the trip alone. Like you, he was concerned about my safety after dark."

Stover snorted. "Don't you never compare one of them sneaks to me, gal! I don't want that whelp to set foot on our property again—is that perfectly clear to you?"

"Yes, sir."

His piercing eyes continued to rake her unmercifully. "And you claim that your dress was ruined before Danmyer got there?"

"Yes, sir. I cleaned off what I could and was about to start the walk for home. That's when he came by and offered to help."

"So you was going to walk home barefoot?"

Marian gulped down her fright. "Yes, sir."

He snorted again. "You'd have been lame for a month."

"Yes, sir."

"It don't seem quite right," he ventured. Marian's heart sank, the dread rising in her throat. "You sure that Danmyer didn't try and get sweet with you? Nothing like that?"

"Absolutely not!" she replied a bit too firmly. Quickly, "He was the perfect gentleman."

"And you will swear to that?"

"You don't believe me?"

"Swear it!" he gave the order. "Swear to me that there was nothing else that went on betwixt you two!"

Marian flinched at his command. Trembling with a mix of anxiety and the cool of the night, she ducked her head and murmured, "I swear, sir, nothing happened."

Stover relaxed visibly. "All right, gal, you get on into the house. I'll put up the team."

Marian had to fight the urge to run toward the house at

full tilt. Instead, she walked as normally as she could to the door. She was besieged by mortification and guilt. Never before had she lied to Stover.

But she hadn't lied, she reasoned. Jerrod had been a gentleman. The fact that she'd had to parade about with only a blanket while her clothes were drying was nothing to be ashamed of. However, she knew that Stover would not understand that, not in a million years!

The sod house was divided into three rooms, with Marian forced to sleep in the same room as her two younger brothers. She pushed the blanket door aside and entered the small cubicle. Quickly, she removed her outer garments. Except for a slight glimmer of light from the next room, it was dark. Even so, she felt self-conscious about sharing a room with the boys. Tommy was sixteen—not exactly a boy any longer—and Brandon was at the curious age of fourteen. Never having any privacy was a strain.

Marian made a swipe over her blankets to make certain there were no spiders or insects, then slipped into bed and pulled the covers up around her shoulders. Relaxing her tired muscles, she listened for Stover to enter the house and go to bed. There was a very brief exchange of words from her parents' room.

Stover dismissing Mom's questions, she guessed. Then the house grew silent and there was only the sound of crickets to break the stillness of the night.

Glancing about, now that her eyes were accustomed to the darkness, she could make out the sleeping forms of her two brothers. She made the decision to ask her mother about a partition of some sort; even a blanket between the beds would add a little privacy. Then, knowing that sleep would still be a long time coming, she closed her eyes and silently said her evening prayer.

# CHAPTER 3

THE SADDLE CREAKED as Jerrod shifted his weight. His back was stiff from the strenuous work of unloading and reloading Marian's wagon. He was well conditioned to work, but it had been an eighteen-hour day.

The travel was slow because of the darkness and the damp trail. Bingo was a surefooted horse, but Jerrod did not risk injury by hurrying. The temperature continued to drop, and he untied the poncho and peeled it from the blanket roll. As he slipped it over his head, he knew he would never think of the poncho in the same way again.

The corners of his mouth curled into a grin as he thought back over the events of the evening. Marian Gates had been the object of his attention for a good many years. The fact that she knew he had watched her from a distance was strangely enticing.

He recalled how she had looked, laid out on the bank, smeared with mud, her arms flung out to the sides from her exhaustive efforts. She had the auburn hair that often denoted a temper, but the fire in her was not only disposition. When her hazel eyes were level as she boldly confronted him, he saw a beauty that went beyond mere appearance. It did little good to deceive himself. He had nursed an infatuation for Marian since he had first set eyes on her.

A depressive mood settled over him at the thought. Stover hated his guts. He hated all of the Danmyer family, their cattle, their horses, their chickens, and even their dogs. Stover's rage over the death of Zeb would never be slaked.

Bingo perked her ears forward, alerting Jerrod. He eased back on the reins and stopped. Someone was on the trail, coming directly at him. Even as his hand touched the butt of his Colt, he relaxed.

"That you, son?" Jake's voice reached him.

"It's me, Pa."

Jake rode up until they were only a few feet apart. "I was starting to worry some. You get lost?"

"One of the Gates family got stuck at the creek crossing. I spent some time helping get a wagon out of the bog."

The explanation caused the man to laugh. "Now, there is the act of a good Samaritan. Are you still in one piece?"

"Yeah. Stover managed to help me keep from getting too high on myself over the act. He wanted to fight."

"That man is about as hard and unyielding as a railroad spike."

"Be tough to have a father like him."

Jake swung about and started his horse moving. Jerrod nudged Bingo into a walk again. They had gone only a short way before his father turned to look at him.

"So which of the Gates did you fish out of the mud— Tom or Brandon?"

Jerrod cleared his throat. "Neither one."

That put an incredulous look on Jake's face. "Not Stover's daughter? He would have killed you on the spot!"

"Figured it might come to that for a minute."

"You got more brass than an army band, son." He grunted. "Either that, or less brains than a patch of daisies."

"She told me that Faron kidnapped Laura and forced her to marry him."

"I believe Zeb made that accusation, before he come gunning for Faron. Tough to admit the truth, that a woman you took in and traveled with for a thousand miles decided on a different man."

"Faron moved away right after the gunfight. I guess it could have appeared that he forced Laura to marry him."

"Laura felt a lot of guilt over the death of Zeb. She never intended to fall in love with Faron. It just happened."

"I told Marian that."

"Oh, Marian, is it?"

"We're on a first-name basis."

"That's good, son. Then, when her pa kills you, she can refer to you by your first name for the final prayer over your grave."

"I've got me a hankering, Pa. I'm going to see that girl again."

Jake's mouth was agape. "You're as crazy as Faron was, son. What is it? Is there some kind of bug that flies about in these Kansas skies that bites a man and makes him loco?"

"I'll figure a way."

"You'll get yourself killed. Stover is no weakling. That man could best a grizzly bear and give it first bite."

"Then I'll win him over."

Jake laughed again, without humor. "Son, that's got to be the most durned fool notion I ever heard of. You might as well try and reason with a coiled rattlesnake. How do you expect to ever win him over?"

"I don't know yet, but there's got to be a way."

"You're letting yourself in for one big heartache, son. You'll end up with a busted heart or a broken head or both!"

"We'll see."

"I'm telling you, Jerry, don't waste your life brooding for a girl like Marian Gates. She's like the moon, bright and purty, but too durn far off to reach."

"I've made up my mind, Pa."

Jake uttered a deep sigh. "All right. I've often said that every man has the right to be a fool *once*."

*        *        *

A ray of sunshine seeped through the wooden shutter on the window and lit the room. Marian was pleasantly surprised to discover that she was alone. She had been allowed the luxury of sleeping late.

She stretched lazily, but dared not remain in bed any longer. Rolling out from under the blanket, she slipped on her old work dress. The thin material was unevenly dyed to a sickly pale yellow, the seams were roughly sewn, and it hung about her shoulders like the flour sack from which it had been created. Other than her Sunday go-to-meeting dress and the soiled outfit she had worn the previous day, the work dress was the full extent of her wardrobe. She glanced downward and grimaced at the way such an outfit detracted from her feminine features. It would be an embarrassment to have Jerrod see her in such a nothing dress.

The thought echoed through her head. *Why do I think of only him and his opinion? I wouldn't want anyone other than family to ever see me in this!*

Wilma must have heard her stirring. She poked her head into the room, and her face displayed a rare smile. "I've got a couple eggs left, dear. Are you hungry?"

"Not really," she answered, keenly aware that their dozen past-their-prime hens did not provide enough eggs for the family's needs.

"I should think you would be starved. You didn't get home in time for supper last night."

"Actually, I had fried fish, a plate of beans, and a half-tin of peaches." She smiled at her mother's raised eyebrows. "When I get stuck in the mud, I do have some good fortune in who comes to my rescue."

Wilma held the blanket that served as the door to one side. A frown rushed into her face, accenting the wrinkles about her eyes and at the corners of her mouth. Marian had grown accustomed to the look. It appeared whenever someone did or said anything that might displease Stover.

"Mr. Gates was unhappy about your coming home so late."

"It wasn't my choice. I was fortunate to get home at all."

"He said that the name of your escort is not to be mentioned in this house. I think we would do well to heed his warning."

Marian felt her temper rise. "The man spent two hours getting my team out of the mud, Mother. He had to unload and reload those posts from the wagon. Then he shared his food with me. He saw me safely home, concerned about my traveling after dark."

"That was chivalrous of him, but he is a Danmyer."

"I know he's a Danmyer. In fact, we discussed Faron Danmyer and Uncle Zeb. His story is a little different from the one I've heard in this household."

"You wouldn't question Mr. Gates about Zeb's death? He would skin you alive!"

"I only wish to know the truth."

"Mr. Gates has told you the truth. Zeb went to get Laura back and was killed for his trouble."

"I'm not convinced that it happened exactly that way."

Wilma shook her head. "Honor thy parents, Marian. It says that in the Good Book."

"Yes, and it also says parents will honor thy children. When do I reach that point? I'm almost nineteen. When will my voice be heard?"

Her mother lowered her head slightly, much the same as when she addressed Stover. She changed the subject. "I've prepared some hot water. We can try and squeeze the two lemons Mrs. Loring gave me the other day. It might be enough to get some of the ground-in dirt out of your dress."

Marian decided the matter of Faron and Zeb was ended. She joined her mother in the chore of washing just about every stitch of clothing in the house. Her part was to rub a hard, coarse bar of lye soap against the material on the scrubbing board. Wilma would rinse the article and then hang it on the clothesline.

After a time, Marian opened a new conversation. "You've never told me, Mother, how did you meet Stover?"

Wilma lifted a thin shoulder and brushed at a strand of ash-gray hair. She stared off into space, as if it took her total concentration to think back twenty years.

"Stover, his father, and mine all worked the coal mines together. Upon Stover's twenty-first birthday, the two of them decided on an appropriate dowry and I was promised to Stover."

"You mean without even knowing him first?"

She gave Marian a sharp glance. "My father was securing my welfare. He attached me to a man he knew to be honest and a hard worker. I was much more fortunate than a lot of girls."

"But didn't you have a courtship?"

"I knew him on sight, and we'd sat together in a Sunday meeting once. He was strong, mature, and very respectful to his elders. He was always willing to help a neighbor or lend a hand to a stranger." She paused, before adding, "If he seems harsh to you or the boys at times, it is because he was raised under a stern hand. It is the duty of the father to see that children are respectful, grow straight, and behave with proper manners."

"I have felt his stern hand," Marian said through clenched teeth. "He used a strap on my bare back, last Christmas Eve, after I took that hayride with the Lorings." She could not keep a bitter resentment from entering her voice. "I had to hold on to the center post in the woodshed, like a bound animal, Mother. I asked Tommy to tell him where I was at. I didn't do anything wrong!"

"You went without permission." Wilma sided with Stover—as she always did. "Some lessons are very difficult. Mr. Gates told me how it hurt him to discipline you."

"Hurt him!" She laughed contemptuously. "He should try it from my side of the belt!"

"He punished you because he loves you, Marian. Most parents discipline their children in the same manner. It is a difficult task to raise children, knowing that a single mistake can cost their life. Parents must determine the steps to take to teach each child the best they know how."

"And then shove their daughter off into the slavery of another man! Mother, he wants to give me to Wolfgang Kruger! I don't wish to marry him. I don't even like him!"

Wilma's face clouded, but there was also helplessness in her expression. She could not imagine standing up to her husband. She accepted his word as law, never questioning it and only rarely seeking to sway his judgment or reasoning. To Wilma, it was unfathomable for Marian to think of questioning his decision.

After a pause, her mother replied. "Love is a romantic notion, my dear, a luxury that only the writers of books can afford. Strength, survival, a man who will provide for you and your children—those are the traits necessary in a husband."

Marian held her tongue because she didn't want to upset her mother. Right or wrong, Stover's word was law in their house. She returned to her work, dwelling on her fate.

Stover and her mother shared their life, but they did not seem to share love. Marian felt two people should laugh together, hold hands, cuddle before the fire at night, and kiss each other at parting. That's what she wanted for her own life.

She stared hard at the dirt around the cuff in Tommy's trousers and rubbed the bar of lye soap until her arms ached. The grime was embedded like Stover's personality—stubborn, hard, unyielding. It was ludicrous for her to resist his will, but she vowed not to end up wed to Wolfgang without having exhausted every possibility.

*     *     *

Jerrod was saddling his horse when three riders entered the yard. He recognized Lyle Harker, the town mayor and banker. Along with him were Keno Dean, who owned the tavern, and Link Peters, the man who operated the general store. The three of them had arrived to open businesses in Eden near the end of the war.

Harker was a portly man, sporting a rather narrow mustache and bushy sideburns that ran down to the bottom of his jaw. He was smooth in the delivery of his words and enjoyed any social gathering that allowed him to give a speech. Jerrod knew little else about him, but the mayor seemed to have a genuine concern for the welfare of the people in Eden.

Keno was an odd sort. He drank to excess, always possessing a bottle or flask of rotgut, but Jerrod had never seen the man drunk. He was thin and wiry. When a sheriff was needed, Keno was the man who wore the badge. A wandering cowpoke had once claimed that Keno had ridden with Quantrill. However, when Keno took exception and called him on it, the man turned tail and ran. No one else had ever come forward with the accusation.

The third man, Link, was one of those men who didn't talk much. He set credit limits for each family and never wavered in his judgment. His best friend was the dollar in his pocket.

Jake had obviously heard the riders. He came out onto the porch, tipped his hat down to shield his eyes from the morning sun, and greeted the three with a raise of his hand.

"Mr. Danmyer," Lyle said amiably. "Good to see you again."

"You too," Jake replied. "What brings you out this way?"

"We are here to represent the businessmen of Eden. As mayor, I have been contacted by some potential land speculators from back east. There is a growing demand for farms, especially where there is access to water."

"That so?"

Link nodded. "Your family owns some eight hundred acres of prime farmland and you are grazing beyond that for another thousand acres."

"Biggest place for miles around," Jake agreed.

"As the mayor pointed out," Link said, "there are some buyers back east who will pay handsomely for prime property. We figured that you might have some land to sell."

"Nope, we ain't got no land for sale, Link." Jake then looked over at the tavern owner. "What's your interest in this?"

"There's a commission for every parcel we can offer up," Keno said.

"Business not too good at the tavern?"

"Always use new faces and their money. We ain't exactly on any main trails here in Eden. I don't make much of a living on a stagecoach each week and a few stragglers."

"Well, I'm sorry, boys, but I can't help you."

Link said, "You might give it a little consideration, Mr. Danmyer. These fellows are talking a fair amount of money here—cash on the table."

"You're wasting your breath." Jerrod spoke up from behind the three men. "Like Pa says, we don't have any land for sale."

Link frowned at the intrusion, but his voice was mellow when he spoke. "This town can grow, but you Danmyers control the flow of the Raccoon Creek by virtue of your property."

"We ain't of a mind to dam up the stream," Jake told him. "The water is there for anyone along its route."

"That's the point. With a dam and irrigation, this community could grow to the size of Dodge or even Kansas City. We could get a railroad spur from the Kansas Pacific Railroad and ship our produce back east. There's a city waiting to be born in Eden."

"If we had wanted to live in a city, we'd have moved to

one to start with, Link. With frequent droughts and bitterly cold winters, the land around here is supporting all the people and livestock it can handle."

Keno produced a small flask from inside his shirt and took a short sip. He did not blink at the burning liquid, but spoke to Harker. "I told you that it would be a waste of time to ride out here, Mayor."

Harker gave an affirmative nod, but Link did not wish to let up. "There are a dozen buyers waiting, Danmyer, begging for land. How about giving us a little help here."

Jake was tired of the conversation and let it show in his reply. "If you need help finding your way back to town, we can show you the road. Other than that, the answer is no."

Jerrod moved around to stand next to his father. He allowed his hand to naturally rest on the butt of his Colt. The three men had come to talk business, but Keno could turn cold in a split second. He had stopped more than one fight in his place by pistol-whipping both patrons.

Link waved his hand in an encompassing gesture. "What about your north two parcels? You only use that for winter feed."

Jake answered, "And when the winter comes, we'll need that store of cut grass and wild wheat."

"Maybe you should see a doctor about your hearing problem, Link," Jerrod ventured. "Sometimes it's only a buildup of wax."

The store owner glared at him. "You three are feeding on prime steak while everyone else in the valley is fighting over a few meager bones. How much land do you need?"

"The question is, how much do *you* boys need?" Jerrod asked in return.

Keno was the one to reply. "I don't need more than my tavern and a friendly bottle." He grinned, but there was a steely glint in his eyes. "But I do need customers to stay in business. The bunch of you here sure don't buy much in my place."

"Get a decent cook," Jerrod told him. "We don't do much drinking, but we'd pay for a good meal now and again."

"It ain't my fault if the Widow Heinrich makes only German dishes. She's the only one who will work for what I can pay."

"Gentlemen," Harker interrupted, "I think our business is finished here. Keno, Link, it is obvious that the Danmyers have no land for sale."

"Easy for you to say that, Lyle," Link growled. "You own the bank. You can charge upward to thirty-percent interest on every dime you lend out. I work on a tight percentage and mostly on credit. I'm struggling to keep from going broke."

Harker frowned. "Link, you would find the same interest at any bank in the state. Where there is a strong possibility of default, I have to charge more to cover the gamble."

"And by virtue of that higher rate, you force those people into folding. Then you can resell their property for a big profit. Yeah, I can see where I should have gotten into the banking business instead of setting up a store."

The mayor's face grew dark. "We didn't come out here to fuss among ourselves. We've wasted a trip."

"Sorry we couldn't help you, Mayor," Jake offered seriously, "but we ain't got nothing to sell."

The mayor lifted a hand in parting. "I understand perfectly. Good day to you, Jake. You too, Jerrod. I'll be seeing you gentlemen."

"So long, Lyle," Jake replied.

The mayor jerked his horse around and kicked it into a lope. He did not sit a horse well, even when it was in a smooth gait. A man confined mostly to a desk and chair, he was out of time with the animal.

"So much for community support," Keno quipped. "I told the mayor that you Danmyers wouldn't be any help."

"Take his example," Jerrod told Keno, "and ride out."

Keno narrowed his gaze. "Best walk softly, Danmyer," he warned. "You don't want me for an enemy."

"Nor for a friend, I'd wager," Jerrod retorted.

Link emitted a sigh of resignation. "It's been a waste of breath to talk to you people."

"Your breath is pretty wasted all right, Link," Jerrod quipped. "Did you have skunk stew for lunch?"

Jake swatted Jerrod's arm, stepping forward to resume the conversation himself. "You done made us an offer and we done said no, Link. I reckon we're through talking."

"It would seem so," Keno replied, but he remained stationary. His eyes were pale green and as lifeless as those painted on a doll. He fixed a stare on Jerrod.

"You got a real keen sense of humor, Jerry," he said dryly. "You oughta think about trying your luck on stage— the next one out of town."

Jerrod smiled. "Now you surprise me, Keno. I always thought you had all the warmth and charm of a sack of smallpox, and here you are, making a jest. Goes to show that we have something in common—we both tell bad jokes."

Keno chuckled, took another sip from his flask, and tucked it away. He halted his motion and flicked his eyes down at Jerrod's gun. "One last thing, Jerry. If it came to a fight, you would be a mite slow getting that snake killer out of its holster. The thong is still in place."

Jerrod met the man's gaze, measuring him, unwilling to show any fear. To counter his statement, he smiled. "I appreciate your telling me about it, Keno."

Keno turned his horse around with slow deliberation. He and Link started back toward town. Within a few minutes, they had caught up with the mayor and were gone from sight.

"You tired of living?" Jake snapped. "What's the idea of

pushing Keno? He's about as deadly as a boot full of scorpions!"

"What do you make of it, Pa?" Jerrod ignored his outburst. "Do you think those three are going to all the nearby farms and trying to buy them out?"

"I wouldn't doubt it. You heard what they said, there's a commission from every sale—more than that if they can pick up one of the farms cheap and resell it themselves."

"Think I'll slip by one of the neighbors in a day or two and see if they made him an offer. You never know when Link and Keno might start pushing a little too hard. If they do, we'll darn well want to do something about it."

"The mayor won't stand for anything like that."

"Harker owns the bank, but Keno and Link can do what they please without his consent. I don't think the mayor pulls much weight against the two of them."

"You could be right, son."

"Link was right about the interest Harker charges. He has busted a few farmers in the past couple years. If he was of a mind to, he could break half the people in the valley."

"The mayor only does what he has to in order to stay in business. Keno and Link might have arrived at the same time, but I've never trusted either of them."

Jerrod waved a hand to chase off a buzzing fly. "I guess there's no harm in them making the farmers an offer for their land."

His father agreed. "Nope. Nothing a'tall. Let's get to work, before Vince comes to complain that we deserted him."

"Get the rifle reloaded, Brandon!" Stover shouted at the youngest member of the Gates family. "You'll get us all killed, standing around with your fingers in your ears! That there target is a man with a gun! If you don't shoot him, he'll darn well put a hole in your gizzard!"

Marian grimaced, watching her little brother. He was the weakling of the family, and not only because of his age. Sickly as a child, he had grown up with a passion for music and enjoying the wonders of nature. He often picked a wildflower to show her and would stop work to watch a bird in flight or the chipmunks chase one another about. He was an unlikely son to a man raised as hard as a drill bit.

"For crying out loud, Brandon!" Stover stomped over to the boy and snatched the weapon out of his hands. "You've got to pull back the bolt! You can't just shove the round down the barrel!"

"Sorry, sir," Brandon whined. "I ain't never loaded this gun before."

"The only thing he's ever fired is the shotgun," Tommy said, sticking up for Brandon.

"All right!" Stover bellowed, pushing Brandon away from the rifle. "If trouble comes, you use the shotgun! Marian!" he said, turning his ire toward her. "It's your turn. If Indians or night raiders come to our house looking for trouble, we'll give them a dose of lead!"

Marian was glad that Tommy had spent some time showing her the workings of the rifle. She missed the big post on her first try, but scored a hit on both her second and third shots. It was enough to satisfy Stover.

"That's good!" He called an end to their practice. "Dig the lead out of the post, Tom. We'll put in a store of ammunition for both guns." He paused, extending a long finger to include all three of them. "And no one moves about alone. That understood?"

"Has there really been Indians sighted?" Marian asked.

"No telling who the enemies are, gal. Someone set fire to one of Andy Brown's fields the other night. Shot at Toby, too."

"Why would anyone do that?"

"Andy didn't know what the reason could be," Stover

said grimly. "The idea is for us to be ready for anything that comes our way. Now get a move on!"

Once Stover was out of earshot, Tommy put a consoling hand on Brandon's shoulder. "If we get some time later, I'll give you a couple lessons on how to shoot the rifle. Now you take the gun to the house. I'll dig the lead out of the post."

"Bet you don't find none of mine," Brandon said sourly. "I never come close to the post."

Marian watched Brandon hurry toward the house with the rifle. The gun looked larger than him.

"Sometimes I feel so sorry for Brandon," she said.

Tommy did not watch his brother. He had a curious look on his face when he spoke to Marian.

"I heard you come home last night," he said. "When I heard voices, I peeked out the shutter."

Marian did not offer a word.

"Stover was in a rage by the time it was dark. If we had owned another horse, he would have set out to look for you."

"I tried to take the shortcut across Raccoon Creek and got stuck to the hubs."

"I saw the dried mud crusted on the wheels this morning. What else happened?"

"Nothing."

"Who was the guy?"

She sighed, expecting Tommy to tease her. "Jerrod Danmyer."

Tommy, however, continued to display a serious mien. "We had company last night, while you were gone— Vernon Kruger. I didn't catch all the words, but he and Stover were discussing your future."

Marian's heart stopped. A cloud of dread swept over her like a shroud of doom. She ran her tongue along her lips, needing the moisture to ask, "And?"

"Vernon said that he was going to add a second house to his place. He has plenty of room, what with them only raising feed for their hogs." Tom sighed. "I expect Wolfgang will come courting one of these next days."

There it was, laid out before her. Marian was unable to focus her eyes, staring out across the field of nearly ripe corn. A vast emptiness spread through her chest, as if someone had pulled her life plug and let the air escape from her lungs.

"Wolfgang ain't so bad," Tommy continued. "He plays an accordion as good as anyone I ever heard, and he ain't ugly or nothing." At her lack of enthusiasm, he added, "Besides, Vernon is about as rich as anyone in the valley. You won't have to worry about your kids going hungry or not having a roof over your head."

Marian wrung her hands. "Yes, but . . . but I don't like him, Tommy! He has such a simpleton laugh. He sounds like a hyena with a feather up his nose!"

"No argument there. Still, Vernon knows a good thing for his son when he sees it, and you're it."

"I'll refuse! I'll run away. I'll go somewhere and find work! If it means starving out on the open plains, I'll not be bound to him."

"Stover would find you, and he would beat you black and blue for going against his will."

"What about you?" she asked, challenging him. "What would you do if he pointed his finger at a girl and said 'There's your wife!' "

Tommy grinned. "Guess I'd decide if I wanted her or not."

"And if you didn't?"

He took a deep breath and let it out slowly. "There will come a day when Stover has to accept me as a man, on even terms. If not, I'll leave. If he won't let me leave, I'll fight him."

"I can't physically fight him," Marian replied. "But it isn't right! I should have some say in my own life."

"Stover sees finding you a husband as part of his responsibility. If you refuse to marry Wolfgang . . ." He let the words hang. "I know the beating you got for going on that hayride. I heard your screams from the shed."

Marian felt an instant shame. It wasn't that he had heard her involuntary cries, for she had also heard his wails on occasion, suffering under the brutal leather strap. The shame was because she had been forced to endure such degradation at her age, compounded by the fact that she didn't feel she deserved such harsh punishment.

"Thanks for telling me about Vernon, Tommy. It will help me prepare for whatever lies ahead."

"If we left together, we might make it on our own, sis. I'm old enough to get a job, and you're a good worker. We could get by."

She offered him a smile of genuine affection. "Thanks, Tom, but I'm not ready to run—not yet."

"I suppose your next move is to keep getting the wagon stuck until the right guy comes along to get you out."

"I didn't do so badly this time."

"Pulled out by a Danmyer?" He laughed at the idea. "You're lucky Stover didn't drag you into the woodshed for that."

"Jerrod was a perfect gentleman. I told Stover as much."

"Bet he took a spoon of castor oil before going to bed, just to get the bitter taste out of his mouth. There you were, waiting for a shining knight to arrive on his white stallion and carry you off to his castle, and you get the most hated man in the household."

"His horse was a mare, and she was black, and her name was Bingo."

Tommy snorted. "A mare named Bingo. That's a real tough name for a horse."

"What do you mean?"

"You'd expect a young man to have a horse named Diablo, Shadow, Widow-maker—something wild, dangerous, or untamed."

"Being a man doesn't mean only being tough and hard. Take Brandon, for instance. He'll never be hard or unyielding like Stover, but he will still become a man."

"What'n thunder you doing over there?" Stover bellowed from the yard. "Get the slugs outta the post and get on back here! We've got a fence to build!"

"Yes, sir!" Tom shouted back, using his knife to dig for the bullets.

Marian stood next to him, her hands cupped together against the wooden shaft to catch the pieces of lead. She allowed a smirk to surface. "That's the man you intend to stand up to?"

Tommy showed his good-natured grin. "Yeah, but not today, sis. Not today."

# CHAPTER 4

JAKE DANMYER STOOD at the head of the table. Vince's wife, Maria, who also was the family cook and housekeeper, poured coffee all around and then took her place next to Vince. Paco and Reuben Sanchez, Maria's two brothers, who both worked for the Danmyers, sat on either side of Jerrod. He was on a stool, leaning against the wall. He sipped the hot brew, as his father took a chair and appeared to gather his thoughts.

"The Brown farm was set afire the other night," Jake began. "It could have been a couple of renegade Indians, or maybe someone getting back at Toby for being a bully." He did not elaborate on that notion, as Paco Sanchez had been Toby's target a few weeks past. The beating had left Paco still troubled by a loose tooth from being hit in the mouth.

Vince asked, "They lose much?"

"One field of corn was wiped out. They are going to have a time of it this year."

"Be a shame to have them fold and move on," Jerrod said sarcastically. "Such nice folks."

That brought a round of snickers, but Jake was not amused. "We have to watch our step, Jerry. It would only take one farmer pointing a finger at us and we'd have the whole town up here to run us out of the country."

"If it comes to settling anything with Toby, I'll do it in person," Vince declared. "He only picked a fight with Paco because he was alone and the smallest guy on our place."

Jake did not pursue that idea. "I ran into the mayor yesterday in town. Max Loring has called a big meeting in town come Sunday. Harker didn't know what it was about, but it had been arranged before the fire. I guess we should have been a little nicer to the folks hereabouts, 'cause we weren't invited."

"Want one of us to sneak into town and try to eavesdrop?"

"No, Vince. We'll let them have their meeting. If it has anything to do with us, Harker promised to pass the information along."

"Other than the run-in with Toby, we haven't had any trouble lately," Jerrod observed.

"You're right, and I don't think we have to be concerned about the meeting. However, we need to start keeping an eye out for anyone snooping around or acting suspicious. I want you all to keep your guns handy, in case there are more of these *accidental* fires."

The group finished their coffee and went about their respective chores. Jerrod could not help but notice that Vince followed him. He finally stopped to see what his brother wanted.

"You were late getting home night before last," Vince said. "And we didn't have fish for breakfast yesterday. You losing your touch with a pole and hook?"

"I ran onto a pilgrim at Raccoon Creek. Had to help get a wagon unstuck and ended up sharing the fish."

"You actually made friends with one of the farmers?"

He sighed, knowing where the conversation was headed. "It wasn't exactly a farmer."

"Oh."

"What do you mean, oh?"

"Nothing," he said, feigning complete innocence. "Only you've been kind of wandering around with your head in the clouds ever since."

"What's that supposed to mean?"

"Oh, I don't mean anything."

"You always mean something, Vince. If you think that something happened between us, you're dead wrong."

"Then this was a farmer gal?"

With a sigh of defeat, Jerrod said, "Yes."

"I reckon it was one of the homely Kruger girls? I mean, there ain't but a couple that are real lookers in the whole valley."

"It was Marian Gates."

"Marian?" he repeated. "She must be close to twenty by this time," he said, grinning, "and cute as a baby's first smile."

"And?"

Again Vince showed an innocent look. "And? Why would there be any *and*? You and the lady spent the night together. That's all there is to it."

"We didn't spend the night together."

"You shared your fish with her."

"It was that or let her go hungry. It took some time to get the wagon out."

"You sure were late."

"I saw her home."

"Silly me, of course you did. Any gentleman would see his fair lady home."

"I didn't say she was my fair lady."

Vince laughed. "With a father like Stover Gates, I should think not. Bet he was as happy as a cow in knee-high clover to see his girl come riding into the yard with a Danmyer at her side."

"I left without shooting anyone and with my own hide intact."

"You were durn lucky, big brother. I wouldn't test my fate a second time, not against an old grizzly like him."

"I'd like to see her again."

Vince groaned, no longer amused by the tale. "I knew it."

"I've a mind to court her."

"That was quick. One night alone, a few hours together, and you think you're in love."

"I already told Pa."

"You didn't!"

"I did."

"You got to be joshing me! I would have heard him laughing."

"It's no joke."

Vince extended his hand. "Been right nice having you as my big brother, Jerry. I'm going to miss you."

"You best hope that when my patience reaches its limit, I miss you too—with the toe of my boot!"

Marian bounced along in the back of the wagon with her two brothers. She was self-conscious about her outfit. She had acquired it when she was fourteen. It once had been too large for her, but now it hugged her tightly across the chest and was too snug at the shoulders. For the past two years, it was the only dress she had for Sunday meetings. It was a simple style made of yellow cotton, now faded, with lace at the collar. Her poke bonnet was white, trimmed with a yellow ribbon so it would match the dress.

Tommy wore Stover's old suit, even though he had not grown into it yet. It was the same suit Stover had worn to marry Wilma twenty years earlier. Brandon also looked a bit awkward, wearing Tommy's hand-me-down suit pants and jacket. The bottom of the trousers was above his ankles and the coat sleeve rode high up on his wrists.

On the wagon seat, Wilma was attired in a heavy black dress adorned with a single lace flounce and supported by several petticoats. Her bonnet had lost its subtle blocking, lying rather flat on her head. Only Stover looked worthy to enter an actual church. His modest suit of black and matching tie had been a gift from the entire family the past Christmas.

The dress and poverty of her family had never bothered Marian to any great degree, for she knew it was people's hearts that made them worthwhile and not their clothing. Still, she was no longer a child. She wished to look more mature, more dignified. The maturity of her build and the cling of the sacklike costume did little to enhance that idea.

Eden rose up before them, a town of a dozen buildings and a single main street. The stage passed through twice each week, but Marian had never been fortunate enough to be in town to watch its arrival or departure.

The buildings consisted of a general store and trading post; a blacksmith shop and livery; the single structure that was bank, recorder's office, city hall, and the mayor's house all in one; a large home that took in boarders and offered baths, shaves, and haircuts; and a tavern that offered food, drink, gambling, and the companionship of an over-the-hill singer-dancer. Scattered nearby were a few homes, mostly of sod, although one or two had some wood for durability.

As they neared Max Loring's livery barn, where the Sunday meetings were held, Tommy lifted a hand and waved at Wolfgang Kruger. Marian immediately looked off in a different direction. If she pretended not to see him, she would not be obligated to wave. Somehow, she had to discourage him. Her one chance was to make Wolfgang decide that he did not want her as his wife. If that came about, Stover would have to accept Wolfgang's decision against any union between them.

However, ignoring Wolfgang was not an easy task. He rushed over to greet the wagon, as Stover reined in the team. Even as the team came to a stop, Wolfgang hurried around to stand in front of Marian.

"Ah-hah, ah-hah!" he laughed in his unmistakable manner, showing a wide, comfortable grin on his face. In his thick, German accent, he greeted her, "I been waiting all morning to have my eyes on you, Miss Marian."

Forcing a degree of cordiality into her face, Marian shook her head. "How have you been, Wolfgang?"

"Ah-hah!" he chortled once more. "I been a lot better now that I see you. Each time, you are more beautiful than the last."

She rewarded him with a smile for his efforts. "Thank you, Wolfgang. That's very sweet."

Stover set the brake, climbed down, then aided Wilma to the ground. Tommy and Brandon jumped over the back of the wagon, while Marian followed after her mother. She hoped that Wolfgang would be lost in the shuffle, but he kept pace with them.

Wolfgang was five or six inches taller than Marian's five-two. He had large, bony hands, big feet, and a large mouth with crooked teeth. His hair was too long to fit his thin face, never combed, and the odor of his family business usually accompanied his boots and clothing.

"How's the pig business doing?" Tommy asked.

"Ah-hah! It be durn good. We gots more sows and weaners than you can throw a stick at."

"Plenty of ham, bacon, and pork for the winter, huh?"

"You bet," he said. "We make lots of money this year."

Tommy caught Marian's eye and winked at her. She knew when she was being taunted and returned an icy stare.

"Mr. Gates," Wolfgang asked her father, as they approached the entrance to the barn, "would it be fine if I sit with your daughter? I promise to be the flawless gentleman."

"Long as there ain't no talking during the meeting."

Marian groaned inwardly at the idea. She would have to keep her hands busy or risk Wolfgang putting one of his paws over her own. Worse, he would spend the entire meeting staring at her, grinning from ear to ear, each time she had the misfortune of looking at him. It was going to be a long, dreadful day.

A good many people were gathered about. There were makeshift benches for Sunday service for the adults; the children sat on the straw-covered floor. A few others leaned against a stall or sat on buckets. Stover led the way over to Vernon Kruger's family and squeezed space enough for all of them to sit down.

Max Loring was more than a blacksmith. He was the spiritual leader of Eden. He had been the one in charge since they migrated from Ohio, holding prayer meetings and giving service over those who died on the journey. Mayor Harker had empowered him as magistrate of Eden so that he could perform other duties to serve the community.

During Sunday services, Mrs. Loring and her husband were like matching bookends. Once each month, she handled the giving of bread and wine, while Max read from Corinthians, relating Paul's description of the Last Supper. She was always there to help, a saintly woman who assumed no reward for her efforts.

"My dear friends," Max began to speak. "May I have your attention, please."

The hush was immediate. Every eye turned to the strong, reliable man. Max, although not an ordained minister, was able to speak parables from the Bible with authority. He was not a domineering man like Stover; there was a gentle calm in his features and sincerity in his voice.

"We will have our regular meeting today. But first, there is another piece of business to put before you, the business of building a school."

There was a smattering of approval from the crowd, but Max held up his hands to stop any discussion. "Mr. and Mrs. Calvin Wilson have agreed to provide instruction. As many of you know, Cal is retired from the army and Ruth taught school at a number of army posts. Ruth claims that her temper might be a bit shorter than in her younger days, but they raised eight children of their own, and she is eagerly looking forward to taking on forty more."

That brought a ripple of laughter. Max relaxed, seeing that there was general acceptance of the proposal. "Doreen and I have helped teach some of your kids the basics over the past few years, but this would be a real school. We will construct a fine wood building at the edge of town, I will make desks and stools, and we shall buy books and educate our children properly."

"Where do we get the money for that?" someone asked.

"Vernon has donated ten pigs to the effort. We will sell them for what money they will bring. A good many others have offered to donate time and personal treasures of value, and we shall have a charity function. I suggest we send word to the nearby towns about our sale. We can have buyers bid for the pigs and other donated goods. We'll have a bake-off with prizes and sell cakes, pies, and crafts. Also, I suggest we have a picnic basket auction. The single ladies from near and far can fix a special lunch, put it in a decorated basket, and the eligible men who attend the sale can bid for their lunches."

Marian experienced an instant delight at the thought. The momentary excitement was shattered at once, as Wolfgang leaned over and whispered, "Ah-hah! I bet you know who will buy your basket!"

"It's settled, then," Max was saying. "The first day of August is the date—that doesn't give you single ladies a lot of time. The baskets will be sold by ribbon color, so the men won't know the owner. Do your best and come prepared for a fun day of charity and goodwill."

Max turned to church functions, singing praise, preaching a short sermon, and offering a prayer for peace and love. As quickly as the meeting ended, Marian was up and out the door. Her effort to escape Wolfgang was wasted, as he was panting at her side, regarding her with his hound-dog eyes.

"Miss Marian," he said, taking hold of her arm. "I've something to say to you." He cleared his throat, as if he had rehearsed the lines. "Would you consent for me to ask of your father's permission that I am able to court you?"

Marian's heart sank. She hesitated, then a spark entered her head. "I'm flattered, Wolfgang," she said, choosing her words carefully. "But surely you wouldn't expect me to agree to anything yet."

"Why not?"

"The charity sale! You heard what Max said about raising money for the school."

"I see nothing that has to do with us."

She ignored his awkwardness with the English language. "I wouldn't be able to put a basket up for bid, if everyone thought that I was spoken for."

His eyes lit up. "Ah-hah, ah-hah!" he said gleefully. "I see what you say. We got to wait till after the sale!"

"Yes."

He again uttered his inane chuckle. "It is not a problem. We got to wait till the big day. Then, when I buy your basket, we show everybody that you be my girl!"

She was fully aware that whoever purchased a lady's basket automatically had the pleasure of her company for the picnic lunch. She forced a smile to her lips, but her heart was crying out in agony. As Wolfgang skipped away happily, she was crushed by the gravity of her fate.

*If only I had some money saved, she lamented to herself. I could have Tommy hire someone to buy the basket—anything to stave off the courtship!* She had managed a reprieve, but it was only until the first day of August. After that, Wolfgang would not be put off!

It was a day later that Tommy plopped down under a sprawling juniper and removed his floppy hat. His hair was pasted to his scalp from the perspiration and afternoon heat. Marian joined in the rest, but sat in the shade of the wagon.

"Be nice to go wading and cool off," Tommy said, "instead of always making this trip only to haul water."

Marian nodded, gazing at the inviting stream. They had filled three of the four barrels, carting two buckets a trip from the creek to the wagon. It seemed to take hours to fill a water barrel and only minutes to empty one.

"If we were smart, we'd bring the cow along with us. That would save us having to fill her trough once."

"Hanna would probably get thirsty from the walk home," Tommy answered. "She would likely empty the trough and we would have wasted the time in bringing her along."

"I suppose you're right."

Tommy waved his hat back and forth to fan his face. He was starting to fill out, but it would be some time before he was full-grown. He caught her looking at him and grinned.

"Saw you and Wolfgang at the back of the wagon. Did he hit you with the big question?"

"I managed to put him off for a few days. After that . . ." She lifted her shoulders in a helpless gesture.

"You going to refuse his offer of courtship?"

"Stover would wail on me until I couldn't walk."

"What about the picnic-basket sale? He'll be sure to buy yours."

"Only if he knows which one it is. I hope—" She stopped in midsentence, shocked to see that a rider was seated at the stream, not a hundred feet away. The rider was Jerrod Danmyer!

Tommy saw the surprise on her face. He jumped up and rushed to the wagon, reaching under the seat for the rifle.

"It's all right!" she stopped him. "It's the man who helped get my wagon out of the mud."

Jerrod let his horse pick her way across the creek. He was again on the black mare, dressed in denim pants and cotton shirt. He wore a gun on his hip, and his hat was tipped low to shield his face from the afternoon sun. He appeared at ease, confident, capable. His poise only added to her insecurity.

Marian rose to her feet, carefully brushed off her work dress, and offered him a timid smile of greeting. "Good day, Mr. Danmyer."

"Fun chore," he said nonchalantly, "hauling water."

"We aim to dig a well one day," Tommy spoke up.

Jerrod measured the boy, then swung his attention to Marian. She detected a gleam in his eyes as the corners of his mouth turned up slightly.

"That you, mud kitten?" he asked. "You're a sight prettier out from under all that mud."

Marian bridled. "You know the name is Marian Gates. This is my brother, Tom."

He glanced back at Tommy. "Do you two always tackle the work the hardest way possible?"

"What do you mean by that?" Tommy asked.

"If you backed the wagon up to the creek's edge, you wouldn't have to carry the water so far to fill the barrels."

"The ground is too soft. We might get stuck."

He gave a tip of his head. "There's some hard-pack down at the creek bend. It's down in a wash, but the ground is plenty solid. You could drive your team right into the middle of the stream and load up in a matter of minutes."

Tommy looked at Marian. She shrugged, not knowing what to say. He picked up his rifle and put on his hat.

"I'll walk down and have a look."

"Just beyond the knoll." Jerrod pointed up the trail. "It would mean driving the team a little farther, but it would save you a lot of steps."

"Wait here, sis," Tommy said. "I'll be right back."

As soon as he was out of hearing distance, Jerrod put his eyes on Marian. She felt a warmth creep up her throat and into her cheeks, while a tingling sensation danced along her spine.

"I've been doing some thinking about you, mud kitten."

"How flattering," she answered curtly. "Such a demure name for a girl you like to think about."

He smiled. "I forget, you allowed that I could call you Marian."

"*Allowed?* You blackmailed me!"

"I've been wondering, Marian, have you been promised as yet?"

"Same as."

"I don't see a ring on your finger, and I haven't heard talk of any formal engagement concerning you."

"Why should it matter?"

"I've a mind to come courting. Think your pa would mind?"

"He'd shoot you on sight."

"That bad, huh?"

"He and Uncle Zeb were very close. I doubt he will ever forgive you for having the name Danmyer."

"I told you Faron fired in self-defense. He had to protect himself."

"It doesn't make any difference to Stover. If you come onto our land again, he'll fill you full of buckshot."

"What about you?" he asked. "Would you be willing to take a ride with me? Have a picnic of sorts? Maybe be my partner at the next dance?"

Marian's heart leapt happily and said *Yes! I'd love to!* but her life was not her own. She controlled the passions that gushed forth. Any relationship with Jerrod was doomed.

"It would be a waste of time, Mr. Danmyer. I will soon be promised to another."

The words stuck into him like a knife, severing his natural confidence to shreds.

"Promised? To who?"

"I don't think I should tell you."

"Afraid I would go after him and run the interloper out of the country?"

She frowned. "To our family, you would be the interloper."

"We agreed to be on a first-name basis—remember?"

"You're changing the subject! You don't know anything about me, and what I know about you is not good."

"All lies," he complained. "I've never hit a woman or child, and I don't kick dogs for the fun of hearing them yelp."

"Regardless, my father would never allow me to see you."

Jerrod stared hard at her, as if attempting to read her feelings. "I'm asking *you*, not your father. Would you be willing to have me come courting?"

It pained her deep inside, but she knew the hopelessness of any positive reply. Lowering her eyes, she gave her head a negative shake. "I'm sorry," she murmured. "It would never work."

Tommy came trotting back toward the wagon. As Marian lifted her gaze once more, she was struck by the dark light in Jerrod's eyes. He gave her a nod of his head.

"I'll say good-bye, ma'am." His voice was dry, void of emotion. "I wish you and your family luck." Then he spun his horse about and splashed across the creek. The black mare opened up, running with the ease and grace of a soaring hawk.

"Sure should have come up with a better name than Bingo," Tommy exclaimed, watching him ride away. "That mare is some kind of horse."

"Yes" was all Marian could manage. Her throat was constricted and tears stung the backs of her eyes.

"The guy was right about the crossing," Tommy continued. "It's on Danmyer property, but we can pull the wagon right into the middle of the creek and load the barrels in a third of the time."

"Stover won't like us being on Danmyer land."

"What we don't tell him won't hurt none."

"If you want to risk it, Tom. I won't miss the extra work."

"So what's the matter, mud kitten?" Tommy teased. "You look like someone just stepped on your toes."

"Don't you ever call me that!" Marian snapped harshly. "I mean it! Not ever!"

The force of her words backed him up a step. She was immediately sorry for flaring up, but it put a look of genuine concern on his face. "I'm sorry, Marian. I didn't know."

"Know what?"

"You really like that guy, don't you?"

"Let's get the water barrels filled," she evaded. "Pa will be looking for us with a switch!"

# CHAPTER 5

ANDY BROWN STOPPED sharpening his ax as Jerrod rode into the yard. He was formed in the same mold as Stover Gates, hard, serious, with an iron constitution and a quick backhand. His son, Toby, was a bully, but not around his father. When Andy was present, Toby was quiet and respectful.

"Danmyer?" Andy gave him a cordial greeting. "What brings you out this way?"

"Heard about the fire, Andy," Jerrod said, stepping down from Bingo's back. "You find out anything?"

Andy set down the ax and squared his body. He was not a tall man, but his shoulders looked three feet across. Squat and constructed low to the ground, he was built for wrestling a bear.

"I spent a couple hours looking around. Found a hot spot that might have been where the fire started."

"We haven't had any lightning lately."

"It was not Nature that set my field afire."

Jerrod understood. "Find any tracks? Anything we might be able to follow?"

"There were some imprints, but not from work boots. Didn't have any heels."

"Like moccasins? You don't think it was Indians?"

"No, but the prints might have been supposed to make someone think along those lines."

"How about horse tracks?"

"Couldn't find any."

"Just curious, Andy, but do you owe any money on this place?"

"Not a cent."

Jerrod considered that. "And no one has made any threats against you?"

Andy glanced across the yard. Toby was planting a post, too far away to hear their words. "I know what you're thinking, Danmyer, that maybe someone has it in for us because Toby sometimes has a heavy hand. Well, I ride the boy hard, see? He works twelve to sixteen hours a day, seven days a week. When he gets a night away, he naturally wants to bust loose. I don't cotton to him picking fights, but he is a physical sort. He likes to mix it up on occasion."

"He pushes too hard sometimes," Jerrod said. "Paco Sanchez wasn't looking for a fight with him the other day. He tried to avoid it."

"Like I says, Toby is a tough sort. When I was his age, I was a tough sort too."

"But you don't believe he crossed someone who wants to get even by burning you out?"

"No, I don't."

"Any conclusions at all?"

"I expect whoever set the fire used coal oil. There was a dark stain on the ground, right where I found those odd prints."

"You tell Keno what you found?"

"I wouldn't give him the time of day, Danmyer. He was with Quantrill when they hit Lawrence, Kansas. You and me were Yankees, and we done some cruel things in the war, burning crops, destroying farms, and such, but we never slaughtered a bunch of innocent people. We never raped women, murdered children, or robbed and plundered, then burned an entire town to the ground."

"And you are sure he was with Quantrill?"

"Heard it from a guy who was drinking at Keno's—the last night I ever set foot in his place. Keno shut him up right quick—a bullet between the eyes does that."

"I heard about the gunfight. I didn't know what it was about."

"Ain't been no one accuse Keno of riding with Quantrill since."

"Wonder if that's why he drinks all the time? Maybe he has a guilty conscience."

Andy spat into the dust. "Man like Keno don't have no conscience."

"With part of your crops gone, how you going to make it?"

"Harker offered to lend me some money to tide me over."

"At twenty percent?"

"Only ten." Andy grinned. "Guess he figures I'm good for it. Any other reason you stopped by, Danmyer?"

"To see how you were doing and to maybe pass along a little advice." He grew serious. "If Toby picks on someone else from our place, I'll be around to settle accounts with him." Staring hard into Andy's flintlike eyes, he could see the man took him seriously, but he was not afraid of threats.

Andy maintained his return look for a long moment, then nodded. "I'll make mention of it to Toby. We got no fight with you Danmyers."

"Glad to hear it, Andy. I'll be seeing you." He swung up onto Bingo and raised a hand in parting. The elder Brown offered the same gesture. Jerrod's warning drew no wrath from Andy Brown—theirs was a simple understanding.

As Jerrod rode down the dust-laden trail, he considered the possible culprits who might have started the fire. The town association had been around to all of the farms, seeking to buy and resell their land. He wondered if one or more of them were not of the mood to take no for an answer.

\* \* \*

The encounter with Jerrod had a disquieting effect on Marian. She rethought their conversation a thousand times. He had offered to come courting and she had said no. Every fiber in her body was in favor of seeing or being near him. But there was no hope. Stover would kill Jerrod before he consented to such a courtship.

There was little time for pining. Replenishing the family store of soap was a time-consuming chore.

She and Tommy fashioned the leach, fitting four boards over a base and slanting them toward the bottom. Brandon burned the last of the hardwood they had in store and gathered the ashes. To the leach, they added straw, then bits of fat and bones that had been set aside, and lastly, the ashes. It was mulched together into the leach, then boiling water was carefully poured over the contents. A container was used to catch the lye that seeped from the concoction. Then the lye was boiled until it formed into a hard lump. Once removed from the water, it was fashioned and cut into soap bars.

With that chore complete, the boys were off to help on the fence. Marian worked alongside Wilma, drawing starch out of some potatoes. After a time, her mother observed her taciturn mood.

"What's the matter, dear? Are you feeling poorly?"

"I'm all right."

"I don't think you've smiled in a week, and you haven't even given any thought to fixing a special lunch for the auction. Aren't you excited about the charity fair?"

"I've got that corn-husk basket I use for my sewing. I suppose I can decorate it for the sale."

Wilma was thoughtful. "It's pretty ragged. Besides, everyone would recognize it as yours."

"What does it matter? Wolfgang is going to buy my basket."

"Would that be so bad?"

She paused from grating the potatoes through the perforated piece of tin. "I really detest the idea of being married to Wolfgang and living on a pig farm. I don't like pigs, Mother. I know someone has to raise hogs, and I love the taste of ham, but . . ."

"I doubt that slopping hogs is any worse than rising each morning to milk a cow. Besides, Wolfgang is well-mannered and would never raise a hand to you. He would make you a good husband."

"I've heard it all before. I have no choice. We women are destined to be slaves and servants all our lives!"

"Marian!" Wilma scolded her. "What has gotten into you?"

"I want some control over my own life, Mother. I believe I should have a say in who my husband is going to be. Is that so wrong?"

"Stover is your father. He is responsible for seeing that you are taken care of. Wolfgang can offer you a home, a life where you won't watch your children die of hunger or from lack of heat in your house."

"I understand all that, but shouldn't I have a choice? Is Wolfgang the only man Stover thinks capable of being my husband? Out of all the men in Eden, he can't be the only man available!"

Wilma was quiet for a moment. When she spoke, her voice was hushed, as if sharing something private. "I've got some strips of black ash stored away. I was going to make a new laundry basket." She paused. "Why don't we use some of it to fashion you a picnic basket instead?"

"Wolfgang will still buy it."

"Perhaps he won't know that it is your basket."

"We have to tie a ribbon on the handle. He knows that I only have one yellow ribbon."

Wilma smiled. "Perhaps we can find another one."

Marian saw something in her mother's eyes. It was a sparkle she had never noticed before, a mischievous glint that bespoke a secret pact.

"But Stover . . . ?"

"Let's not trouble him with the project," Wilma said quietly. "He has so many other worries. We shouldn't concern him with something as trivial as your charity basket."

"You mean it?"

"We've got a hen that hasn't laid an egg in a week. With a bit of my special seasoning, she would fry up as tender as melted butter. With some rolls, baked potatoes, and bread pudding, your basket would be the finest meal in the bidding."

Marian wrapped her arms around her mother and hugged her tightly. In her entire life, Wilma had never opposed Stover. This action was as close as she had ever come to taking Marian's side.

There were races, games of stickball, and horseshoe-pitching contests. The bake sale also included a judging, with ribbons for the best in a dozen categories. Stover was a fair hand at tossing horseshoes and entered that competition. He was in the middle of a game when Max Loring announced that it was time to began the auction for the basket sale.

Max and his wife called for all of the unattached young ladies, widows, and spinsters to bring forth their baskets. Minutes later, the bidders and a crowd of onlookers gathered for the fund-raising event.

Marian held out a slight hope that Wolfgang might be involved elsewhere, but he arrived before the first sale. She stood with the other basket owners and awaited her fate.

"All right, gentlemen!" Max quieted the crowd. "Looks like a fine turnout for the picnic lunches." He displayed a winning smile. "And I can tell you, I'm getting mighty hungry, smelling all of this wonderful food. Wish Doreen would let me bid on a couple of these myself."

The jest relaxed the crowd. Marian held her breath, as Max picked up the first basket. Several bids later, it sold, and Max moved on to the next. He auctioned off a half dozen, but he passed over hers. Any hope she had about her basket being a secret was crushed. Wolfgang had not offered a single bid on any of the others, but when Max finally picked up her picnic lunch, Wolfgang began to dig into his pocket.

Max peeked under the cloth covering and inhaled deeply. "Fried chicken!" he exclaimed. "And it looks mighty good."

Marian swallowed; her heart seemed lodged in her throat and her future seemed black as a moonless night. Even as Max lifted his hand to start the bidding, Wolfgang was laughing his inane chortle.

"Ah-hah! I bid on this one. Three dollars, Mr. Loring. I bid three dollars!"

It was over. Marian's prospects had been brutally slapped down. Three dollars was more than Stover had spent at one time since leaving Ohio. As not one of the other baskets had sold for such a high price, there was virtually no chance that anyone would—

"Three and four-bits!" a second voice offered.

Wolfgang craned his neck, shocked that someone had bid against him. "I say four dollars!" he cried.

Marian searched the crowd but was unable to see who had raised the bid. She held her breath, afraid to let optimism enter her being. It was only a single bid. Whoever had made the offer surely wouldn't be able to compete with Wolfgang.

"And four-bits!" The quiet words reached her ears once more.

Max showed a wide smile and said gleefully, "This is more like it! Four and a half to you, Wolfgang."

"Five dollars!" he shouted. "Five dollars!"

"And four-bits," came the reply again.

Marian could not contain her curiosity. She rose up onto her toes to try and see over the crowd. The bidder was too far back in the crowd. Max was on a platform of sorts, but he gave no indication as to who was doing the bidding. He kept pointing from one man to the other. There was a familiar ring in the second voice. Her heart was suddenly active, palpitating with renewed vigor. She waited, anxious and fearful at the same time.

"I am bid ten dollars!" Wolfgang nearly shrieked, holding the money up over his head, waving it triumphantly.

"It is now ten dollars!" Max repeated the sum eagerly. "Do I have another bid?"

Marian wrung her hands. The silence was enough to shatter her straining ears. Had the price gone too high? Was she doomed to share her basket—and possibly her life—with Wolfgang?

"Ten dollars?" Max announced again. "The price is ten dollars. Do I hear—"

"Twenty dollars!" came the soft reply.

Max stopped with his mouth open. The bid prompted wide-eyed surprise and shocked expressions from the crowd. It was the equivalent of a month's wages for a single lunch basket. Max attempted to speak, but first had to clear his throat to get the words out. "Twenty dollars!" he declared, unable to hide his surprise at the outrageous price. "We have twenty dollars!"

Wolfgang whirled about and shouldered his way out of the room, his face red and contorted with rage and humiliation. Several eyes followed after him, but the bulk of attention was directed to the rear of the group, all seeking to get a look at the big spender.

"It appears that we have a sale," Max sounded off. "Sold for twenty dollars!"

Jerrod made his way forward. Most of the crowd gave him wide passage. One or two even patted him on the back as he passed. He reached the table and dug out the money.

"This is very generous of you, son." Max was jubilant. "Twenty dollars will be a big help toward our goal."

Jerrod handed him the money and displayed a subtle grin. "When you said it was fried chicken, I knew I had to have it. I hope its owner is a good cook."

Several of the people nearby laughed. Max handed him the basket and nodded in Marian's direction.

"Your lovely hostess is Miss Marian Gates. I'm sure that you will be more than satisfied."

Jerrod waited expectantly. Marian commanded her legs to work and walked in his direction. She felt the crimson flood suffuse her face a darker shade of red than the ribbon on her basket. All eyes followed her over to Jerrod's side. The two of them left together, as Max drew forth another basket to sell.

"A bid of a dollar or two is going to sound very small, after what you paid for my basket," Marian whispered. "I can't believe anyone would give twenty dollars for lunch!"

"It is for a worthy cause, and"—his voice grew as smooth as velvet—"I was buying your company, not the lunch."

She did not respond to that, confused, embarrassed, uncertain. Instead, she addressed a real concern. "Stover is going to be furious. I'm quite certain he told Wolfgang which basket was mine."

"Not very sporting of him."

"So how did you know?"

He switched the basket to his left hand, offering her his right arm. "Easy," he answered, as she awkwardly looped her arm through his. "When I saw Wolfgang bid, I knew it was your basket."

"Who told you about Wolfgang?"

"Do we have to talk about him?"

Marian was self-conscious, walking arm in arm with a man. It seemed more intimate than holding hands.

"So where are the boundaries for our meal?" he asked.

"No one mentioned it. For both our sakes, it had best be out in the open."

He grinned, tipping his head toward another couple

from the sale. "How about we stay in sight of that pair? They look like good witnesses for your defense."

Marian laughed at that. It was the first time she had felt so good in days. In fact, she wondered if her feet were even touching the ground.

Jerrod spread out a cloth for them to sit on, while Marian gathered her senses. They sat side by side, and she removed the contents of the basket.

The meal was delicious, but Marian hardly noticed the taste of the food. She was enthralled by Jerrod's smile, his every word, his simple presence. It was something of a disappointment to finish the bread pudding her mother had helped to prepare for dessert, as it marked the end of the meal.

"Worth twice what I paid," Jerrod remarked. "Did you cook all of this by yourself?"

"My mother helped," Marian admitted. "She has always had a knack for cooking."

In a subtle motion, Jerrod's hand slipped over her own. She should have pulled away, but she enjoyed his touch. With a dreamy expectation, she risked looking into his sky-blue eyes.

"Beautiful, and a good cook too. What a prize you are."

The words warmed Marian to the marrow, but she retained her poise. "Wolfgang has probably told Stover that someone else bought my basket by this time. He will be coming to put an end to our picnic together."

"I've a mind to court you, Marian," he told her firmly. "You are everything I could want in a woman."

"Stover would never allow it."

"I won't be swayed by what Stover wants or thinks. My concern is for you. What do you say?"

"I told you . . . I can't."

" 'Can't' is not a word I recognize, mud kitten. It's either yes or no, will you or won't you?"

"It's hopeless," she murmured. "I can't go against Stover's wishes."

"I'm going to take that as a yes."

"You make it difficult to say no."

Jerrod leaned close to her, only inches away. His eyes were pools of passion, his voice coercing, exciting. "I'm going to kiss those inviting lips of yours, Marian. If you have any feelings for me, I'll know it."

She rotated her head slightly from side to side in protest. Yet, even as she was summoning forth the required effort to resist his overwhelming charm, his mouth pressed against her own.

The world was suddenly silent, forgotten. Marian's good sense screamed at her to resist, but there was magic in Jerrod's kiss. She was enthralled by the warm, sincere touch of his lips, swept away on a cloud with wings, soaring high above—

"Danmyer!" a booming voice roared. "What in Sam Hill are you doing to my daughter!"

Marian wrenched away so quickly, she fell back onto her elbows. Before she could gather her reasoning, Jerrod leapt to his feet to face her father.

Stover strode toward them, his rock-hard knuckles locked into tight fists. "Danmyer!" he snarled. "I told you to never come near my girl again."

Jerrod stood his ground, braced for an attack, but he did not assume a fighting stance.

"I aim to court your daughter, Mr. Gates," he replied evenly. "I prefer to have your blessing, but with or without it, I intend to compete for her hand."

"You got straw for brains, boy! Get out of my sight!"

"Like I said, I'm going to court your daughter."

Stover's bony fists came up. "Over my dead body, Danmyer!"

Jerrod raised his own guard. "If need be, it can sure

enough be over your unconscious body, Gates. You ain't going to trod over me like one of your kids."

"You think you're a big man, Danmyer. Well, let's see what you're made of." Stover closed in, big hands clenched and raised in front of his chest, ready to fight.

A crowd had quickly gathered to watch, but the sound of a charging horse came into their midst. Everyone paused to look at the new arrival. It was a sight that diverted the attention of everyone, including Jerrod and Stover.

The horse was lathered to the point of exhaustion. It staggered to a stop and nearly went to its knees. The boy atop its back was no more than eighteen, covered in dust, his eyes wide with excitement. He slid down to the ground, his mouth open, drawing in gulps of air.

"It's my cousin from Colby Flats!" one man exclaimed. "Rudy! What's going on? Did you ride that horse at full gallop for the seventy miles betwixt there and here?"

"Yonder!" the boy gasped, pointing over his shoulder. "They've . . ." He panted to catch his breath. "They've taken flight with the wind!" He waved his arm frantically back in the direction he had come. "Gotta gather everything you can. Protect your food and grain!"

"What in tarnation is that boy talkin' about?" one man asked.

"Look!" a woman cried out. "A storm is coming!"

Rudy shook his head. "It's a storm all right, one like you never seen in your life. Get yourselves home and save what you can. You don't have much time!"

Everyone paused to stare for a minute. In the distance, there appeared to be a massive cloud that stretched as far as the eye could see in either direction, a mile-high dust storm that moved across the prairie. But it was not dust—it was alive!

# CHAPTER 6

THEY CAME ON the wings of the wind and fell to earth like a downpour of rain. Millions upon millions of locusts darkened the sky. They pelted downward onto the crops, the few trees, and every blade of grass, an indestructible ocean of grasshoppers that devoured everything in their wake. An eerie buzzing filled the air, a combination of their fluttering wings and the sawing action from their voracious eating.

The Gates family had reached the house only moments ahead of the horde. With the team still standing in harness, Stover was down and shouting orders.

"Tommy! Brandon! Grab some sacks and fill them with corn! Marian, you move the grain from the shed into the fruit cellar. Use buckets, jars, anything you can find."

It was a race against the devil's spawn. The hoppers fell from the heavens, landing on everyone's backs and in their hair, crawling under their clothes and down their necks. The Gates men tied strings about their trouser legs to prevent the insects from climbing up their legs. Marian donned a scarf to keep them out of her hair, and continually swatted the creatures off of her arms and clothing.

Stover rounded up a bucket of lamp oil and fashioned himself a torch. As the three children hurried to store what they could into the fruit cellar, he used the burning torch to keep the hoppers at bay. It was a hopeless task.

Gathering shovels and boards, they crushed thousands of the wretched insects. If anything, it only incited more and more of the locusts to surge forward.

Marian retreated to the house to help her mother. Wilma

was shoving cloth into the cracks around the windows and doors, trying valiantly to keep the hoppers out. When Marian entered, Wilma stopped long enough to brush the grasshoppers from Marian's clothes and help her kill the ones that had crawled up into the folds of her dress.

Wilma shouted over the noise of the insects. "Shove a blanket under the door and help me stop up the cracks. We have to keep them out of here."

"The little buggers are five or six inches deep out there! It's like wading through a swamp of leeches!" Marian lamented. "They're stripping every bit of our crop, every blade of grass. We can't even slow them down!"

While Tommy and Brandon shoveled dirt over the wooden door of the fruit cellar, Stover used a pitchfork and tossed straw all around the entrance. Then he used the remaining lamp oil and set fire to it. The bodies of the locusts nearly doused the flames. The live hoppers crawled over the bodies of the dead, a swarming mass that could not be stopped.

The three of them stomped and crushed thousands under their heels, they beat at them with shovels, but it was like trying to bail the ocean with a teacup. The seething mass covered everything as far as the eye could see. They not only chewed up the crops and grass, but attacked tool handles, gnawed on the wagon bed, the harness and straps, the boards on the shed, and even the wood portions of the house. It was impossible to fight such an overwhelming and indestructible wave of locusts.

As dusk covered the land, Stover allowed that they had lost the fight. He and the boys withdrew into the house. Marian and Wilma hurried to shut the door. The next few minutes were spent chasing about and killing the hoppers that had come in with the men.

Stover collapsed into a chair and pulled off his hat. His hair was soggy with perspiration, matted to his head, his face stained with sweat. He suddenly appeared years older, a forlorn expression in his sullen eyes, mouth drawn tight.

The hopelessness of the situation sat on his chest like the weight of the world.

"We're beat," he muttered. "By the time this pestilence is finished, there won't be a single bit of grain or a kernel of corn left. Everything we've worked for—ten years of sweat and blood—is gone."

"What'll we do?" Tommy asked. "How are we going to make it through the winter?"

"I don't know, Tom. If the hoppers don't get into the cellar, we might have enough to weather through."

"The dirt we piled on top of the door ought to protect it for a spell. I don't know for how long, though. Them hungry vermin are even eating one another."

"What if they decide to eat us?" Brandon wanted to know. "You think them hoppers would turn to eating human flesh?"

"Don't worry, Brandon," Marian replied. "They don't eat meat."

"I seen them eating each other!"

"Only the portions that contain food. You notice they haven't tried to eat the horses or our cow."

"We're safe in here. The house walls are sod and near two foot thick," Stover reminded them all. "We'll take turns during the night, keeping the wretched devils out of here. So long as they don't eat their way around the door or windowsills, we should be fine."

Tommy said, "There's grass on the roof. If they get past the sod, they might reach the wooden slabs."

"We'll keep a fire going, so they don't come down the chimney. As for the slabs, they won't get past the layer of dirt to reach those. We should be all right."

Wilma served up some beans and hard rolls. They ate in exhausted silence, listening to the steady hum of the working jaws, legs, and wings of millions of locusts.

"Where'd they come from?" Brandon asked no one in particular. "How did there get to be so many of them?"

Stover did not try to answer the question. "You kids go

to bed. I'll wake Tom in a couple of hours. Tom can wake Marian, and so on. The one on guard can keep the hoppers out."

"What if they eat through the door?" Brandon asked.

Again Stover ignored the question. "I have a bucket of machine grease by the door. Smear some on the rags, before you shove them into the cracks. Ordinarily, these critters won't try and eat through grease. It might slow them down a little."

"They don't ordinarily show up five and six deep for a hundred miles in three directions, either," Tommy said. "Let's hope we don't run out of rags and grease before they move on."

"You kids get off to bed. Come morning, we'll rebuild the defenses around the cellar and the house. We also might have to move the water barrels into the house. Whatever we do, we will all need some rest."

Marian led the way. When she reached her bed, she removed the blanket and shook out several hoppers. She squashed them with a vengeance and decided not to remove her shoes or clothing. She wanted something between her and the locusts, should they come crawling into her bed during the night.

"Turned out to be some day, huh?" Tommy asked.

"It's a nightmare."

"Even the picnic?"

Marian eyed him suspiciously. "I've been meaning to ask you, Tom. How do you suppose Jerrod knew which basket to bid on?"

"You should have asked him."

"He said he waited until Wolfgang began to bid."

He arched his brows in innocence. "There you go."

"How did he know about Wolfgang? I didn't tell him who was trying to court me."

"Oh."

"You told him, didn't you."

It was more a statement than a question, and Tommy had never been a good liar. He sighed in defeat. "Yeah, I told him. When I seen Stover whispering to Wolfgang, I knew the deck was being stacked against you. I figured that my telling Jerrod was only allowing for both men to have an even shot."

"You might have caused a fight between Stover and Jerrod. I wouldn't like having two men fight over me."

"So you're mad at me, huh?"

"It was a dangerous thing to do."

"Are you saying that you didn't want a Danmyer bidding on your basket?"

"You saw how angry it made Stover. We could have both ended up out in the shed, taking a beating."

"Maybe you would have thought it was worth it."

"What do you mean by that?"

A light danced in his eyes. "It so happens I was there in time to see you kissing Jerrod."

"I didn't kiss him! He kissed me! I was too surprised to react!"

"Appeared to me that you *were* reacting," he teased.

"Tom! I didn't give him permission to kiss me. I told him no!"

"And real forceful too, I'll bet. Guess it was the angle I was at, but I couldn't see the armlock he had on you."

"I didn't have time to fight. It all happened too suddenly."

"And that's why you didn't see us coming? It was so sudden that you up and shut your eyes!"

Marian swept the bed one last time, making sure it was not infested with hoppers. Then she wrapped the blanket around her and slumped down onto the cot.

"Go to bed. We've got a major war to fight against these lousy insects tomorrow."

"Sure," Tom quipped, "though I doubt that I'll have the same pleasant dreams as you, sis."

"You seen it?" Brandon asked Tommy in a whisper. "Marian really locked lips with that Danmyer guy?"

"You shut up, too, Brandon!" Marian snapped. "Both of you, go to sleep!"

The two boys laughed. It was an odd sound, considering the writhing mass of hoppers that covered the ground for miles around. In spite of the dire predicament, Marian had to smile. She let them enjoy their teasing. The day had produced a memory that she would relive a thousand times. In fact, she wished to recall every detail of the picnic, every word, every moment. Most of all, she would cherish the memory of Jerrod's kiss.

"We've no choice, Pa," Vince repeated Jerrod's idea. "Faron can find us enough range for our herd."

"The blasted hoppers cover the land as far you can see in any direction," Jake reminded them both. "What if you get fifty miles and there is still nothing but grasshoppers? What if you can't reach water or grass?"

"How long can they survive on the barren ground this pestilence is going to leave behind?" Jerrod asked. "The creek is filling up with dead hoppers and their leavings. The cattle won't be able to drink it by tomorrow."

"We'll have that same problem for ourselves in a day or two," Vince said. "We only have that one old Halladay Standard windmill to provide our drinking water. It doesn't produce enough to support all of the livestock too."

Jake rubbed his jaw, thoughtful for a moment. "All right, boys," he finally agreed. "Vince will stay here with Maria and myself. Jerrod and the Sanchez boys can drive our herd of cattle to Colorado." He stared out the window at the disgusting yellow-brown mass. It undulated with uncountable insect bodies, comparable to the wind rippling the tips of tall winter-dead grass.

"Where in heaven do you think they all came from?"

"I expect they didn't originate from heaven, Pa."

"Whatever, we better go ahead with your idea and get the cattle moving. If you can't outrun this swarm, it might mean the death of every steer we own."

Jerrod gathered up enough grub for a week, then donned his rain slicker to protect him from the horde of locusts. He tied his trouser cuffs about his boots, tucked his hat down tight, and went out into the thriving multitude of hoppers.

His every step crushed bodies underfoot. The ones that took flight caused a small blizzard in all directions. It was unlike anything Jerrod could have conceived in his most bizarre nightmares.

It was a battle to saddle the horse. Bingo was a well-trained horse, but she stomped her feet and danced about, trying to be rid of the insects. The hoppers were everywhere, chewing on the blanket, the bridle, and the saddle straps. Jerrod shook them off, only to have them land on him, their sticky feet clinging to his slicker and even on his exposed arms and face. He gritted his teeth and shouted orders to the two Sanchez boys.

Once atop Bingo, he directed the other two riders. Paco managed to get the team and wagon ready and they started out to the herd. The moving hooves of the horses disturbed the multitude of hoppers, causing them to take flight. The result was a swirling tempest from which there was no escape. The horses ducked against the blinding storm and continually swatted with their tails and shook their manes to rid themselves of the pesky insects. As Jerrod rode, there was a constant *thud, thud, thud* as the locusts bounced off his protective clothing.

Reuben came close enough to speak. His sombrero was covered with dozens of hoppers, all trying to devour the hat right on his head. "It is like the end of the world!" he cried.

"You think this might be the wrath of God?"

He crossed himself. "I pray not. I have some sins to atone for yet."

"We'll push the herd all night. If we don't get beyond these filthy vermin in two days, the cattle will die for lack of food and water."

"The hoppers came with the wind. While they are on the ground, eating everything in sight, we can gain some distance on them. If they rise up in flight, we might be headed right into their path."

"The Colorado mountains should be a deterent to them. You seldom see a grasshopper above the timberline."

Reuben's head bobbed up and down. "Yes, but can we reach pine trees before the cattle die of thirst or hunger?"

Jerrod had no answer to that. All they could do was try.

Marian grabbed hold of a hopper that landed on the back of her neck and threw it to the floor of the sod house. Before it could escape, she stomped on it hard. "Damn!" she swore in frustration. "They're like the blowing dust from a sandstorm. The rotten cusses fill your senses like the sickening odor of a skunk. You can smell them, they blind you when you try to walk, their buzzing is enough to drive you mad! I can even taste the filthy parasites in my mouth!"

Wilma patted her arm. "There is nothing we can do but hold out until they move on."

"It's been three days!" Marian cried. "How much longer is it going to last? When will they leave?"

"Only God knows that."

"What is left for them to eat? The cornfield is a few naked stalks and bare ground. They've stripped the bark and branches from the few trees. There is nothing that they haven't devoured or destroyed. I can't sleep at night, afraid the hoppers will come to feed on me!"

"We have to be strong, dear."

"How are we going to live, Mother? We weren't able to save enough provisions to hold us till next harvest."

"Stover will find a way."

Marian fought the heavy blanket of gloom, but the air was oppressive, filled with the never-ending locusts. The can of axle grease was gone, and they had been forced to use their own clothes to fill the cracks between the doors and windows. They had only one water barrel that wasn't tainted. Stover and Tommy had gone to the stream for more water, but came back empty. Raccoon Creek was thick and brown in color from hopper excrement and bodies. Their cow and the team were sick from trying to drink it. The lamp oil was all gone, having been used to keep a fire around the fruit cellar. If they lost that hold, they were destined to starvation.

"Here come your brothers. Get the broom and stand by the door. I'll brush the boys and you kill the hoppers."

"I'll kill them," she vowed. "I wish I could be a giant for a day and had a swatter the size of a railroad car. I'd smash the life out of every last one of the filthy little devils."

The door was cracked wide enough to allow Tommy and Brandon to enter. Even that opening provided time for dozens of insects to pour into the room.

Wilma slammed the door shut. The hoppers flew to the cupboards, toward the flour barrel, and sought any scrap of food. Once the boys were brushed down, the four of them spent fifteen minutes destroying the elusive insects.

"Stover is going to ride the horse into town and see if there are any airtights he can buy at Mr. Peters's store. He said that if we wait until the hoppers take flight, there might be a run on the trading post for food."

"If these locusts got into the store, Link might not have anything to sell," Wilma replied. "Besides which, Stover don't have but a couple dollars saved. He can't buy much with that."

"Reckon he knows that, Ma."

She sighed. "I hope he hurries back. He's the strongest one among us. We need him."

Marian felt a twinge of conscience. Her mother was right about that. Stover was a hard man, strict and regimented, but as dependable as daylight. He had always provided for his family. When times were hard, he often worked sixteen hours a day and then would gather wood, hunt, and fish on Sunday. He never rested while they needed food or heat for their shelter. She had often criticized his lack of compassion or affection, but he showed his love by his own sacrifice. It made her ashamed that she had thought or spoken poorly of him.

"Going to be tough on some of the others," Tommy said. "The Browns had already lost some of their crop to the fire. I heard Andy say they were forced to borrow against next year's harvest."

Wilma nodded in agreement. "A good many of the farmers have borrowed money on this year's crop. I don't think Mayor Harker has enough capital to continue to extend credit on bare ground."

Brandon's face twisted in a frown. "You think he would call in all the notes? Them folks would lose their homesteads."

"I don't know. There are buyers waiting for good land. You recall Mr. Harker and Link came by with an offer to buy our land. I'd say this will give them the chance to get a lot of places for rock-bottom prices."

"Nice to know that someone is going to profit off of these slimy pests," Marian said sarcastically. "Guess the bloodsuckers of the world stick together."

"Mr. Harker has always been there to help, Marian," Wilma replied. "He has helped promote growth and lends money to needy people. A good many of our neighbors wouldn't be here except for his help."

"Yeah, but what about Link Peters?" Tommy said.

"He can't give endless credit at his store or he would go broke, too."

"You can bet he'll be a rich man once this is over. All he has to do is cease giving credit. With Harker about broke, the only way for the farmers to get even will be to give up the deed to their place and move. He can resell their farms to those people back east."

"What real option does he have? He is a businessman. Either he goes broke or the farmers go broke. It's that simple."

"Ma, if Satan himself walked into the room, you'd likely find a good trait or two about him."

She smiled. "Everyone has their good side, Tommy. If you only look for the bad, that's all you will see."

"Guess my eyes aren't as good as your own, Ma. I don't see Link Peters as any better than those hoppers out there, grabbing all he can get, no matter who it hurts."

Wilma dismissed the matter. "Marian, pick out a couple of the worst-looking potatoes from the bin. I'll put together something for dinner that will keep until Stover returns."

"Sure, Ma," she replied. Then she paused to step on a half-dead hopper. "Want to fry up some of these critters too?"

"No." She was curt. "I'd like to boil every last one of the wretched little buggers in oil, but I would never eat one."

"Guess you were wrong, Tom," Brandon quipped. "Even Ma don't see nothing good about these hoppers."

Tommy grinned. "I stand corrected."

# CHAPTER 7

FARON SAT ON the back of his claybank mare and looked over the cattle. They were crowded around the drainage pond, drinking as if they would never slake their thirst.

"The report was in the newspaper yesterday, Jerry," he said. "The locusts seem to have united from back in the Dakotas and are moving across Iowa and Kansas. They appear headed in the direction of Texas. The body of the mass is reported to be a hundred miles wide and three hundred miles long. One account measured the swarm at nearly a mile in height."

"They sure enough arrived like the biggest storm cloud I ever saw," Jerrod replied. "They blackened the sky and swooped down like a downpour of hail."

"Most of the news arrived by train. The engineer reported that the tracks got so slick with the dead bodies of those hoppers that the crew had to get out and throw sand on the rails to keep moving. When the train pulled in, the insect remains were a couple inches deep in some of the cars."

"We rode solid for the better part of two days to get ahead of them," Jerrod said. "We kept pushing for fear they would take flight and overtake us."

"Bit of a rain storm building today. Maybe the cool air will force them to swing south of us."

"What about the herd? Is it going to be a problem?"

"I know a fellow east of here that has plenty of grass for grazing. It will mean borrowing against my place to pay for use of his ground, but we'll get by."

"Thanks, Faron."

"You look beat, Jerry. My foreman can handle your cattle. You and the boys come with me. Laura will fix us something to eat, and the three of you can get some rest."

"I won't argue with you there. It's been a long, hard drive."

As they rode together, Faron appraised Jerrod. "You look good, little brother, all growed up. I haven't seen you since you went to fight in the war. You were only a kid of sixteen then."

"A real waste of human life there, Faron. If I never see a man die again, I won't feel I missed anything."

"I was the eldest. It should have been me."

"You were never a fighter," Jerrod said without censure. "The maiming and killing would have destroyed you. I watched men die from every kind of ailment imaginable."

"Sounds pretty gruesome."

"Fever, dysentery, infection from the smallest of wounds. More men died of that sort of thing than were killed in the fighting. I only fought in two or three actual battles, but fully a third of the men I served with died."

"High price to pay to get us all under one flag."

"Guess every country has to sort out their own problems that way on occasion. Maybe we'll be a stronger nation because of it."

Faron grinned. "I recall that you were always an optimist."

"A what?"

"It means you have a positive outlook, always think things will turn out for the better."

"Reckon it don't take any more energy to think that way, rather than always looking for the downside of something."

"Do you see anything positive in this plague of locusts?"

"You got me there, Faron. All I can see there is misery, destruction, and death."

They reached the Danmyer home and put up their

horses. Paco and Reuben ate their meals in relative silence and went to the bunkhouse for some rest. Jarrod remained at the table as Laura cleared away the dishes.

"How's Pa holding up?" Faron asked, leaning back in his chair. "He still going from daylight till dark?"

"Never runs out of energy."

Faron cocked his head toward the yard. His two children were playing at the water trough, floating a makeshift sailboat back and forth.

"I know that feeling. Little Jerrod and Ellery never seem to run short of energy. Did I tell you that they both can read and write?"

"Already?"

"Got a school a couple miles from here. Jerrod is eight and Ellery is going on seven."

"Time does fly."

Faron scrutinized his brother. "What about you, Jerry? Now that Vince has found himself a wife, you ought to be looking to start your own family, too."

Jerrod smiled. "I think I've found a prospect, but it's going to take a whole lot of work to snag her."

"You mean because you're the ugly one of the family?"

Jerrod laughed. "No . . . because the girl is Marian Gates."

He could have said Satan's daughter and it would not have caused a more distressed look. Both Faron and Laura stopped to stare at him.

"You and Marian Gates?" Laura murmured. "I'll bet Stover has some choice thoughts about that."

"I said it would be a chore."

"Never happen," Faron declared. "Stover will kill you first."

"He did threaten me with something to that effect."

Laura sat down at the table. It was not as if she wished to continue the conversation, more that her legs would no longer support her.

"Dear God," she whispered.

Faron's expression was one of deep concern. "You recall that Vince met Maria when he came to visit with us a couple years back?"

"I remember."

"So let me introduce you around. There are some real nice young ladies about. You can't really think Marian is the only girl for you?"

"I've made up my mind."

"Stover won't have it," Faron said again. "He won't."

"Maybe he's softened up some since you two left."

Laura stretched forth her hand and placed it on Jerrod's arm. There was a disturbing expression on her face, one of agony and regret.

"Maybe we should tell him, Laura," Faron encouraged her.

"Tell me what?" Jerrod asked.

Laura appeared to sort her words carefully, as if it pained her to think about what had transpired years earlier. When she spoke, her voice was little more than a whisper.

"Stover was ten years older than Zeb. He was not only a big brother, he was like Zeb's own father. It was Stover who made arrangements for me to travel with the Gates family to Kansas. He came to my aunt and promised to watch over me. He did not actually suggest that I was to marry Zeb, but it was a strong consideration."

She paused, as if swallowing her guilt. "He knew there would be few women for the men out on the new homesteads. I was eager to start my own life and joined the family to come west with them. Stover was careful to allow me my privacy and let me feel as if I always had a choice about the arrangement.

"Zeb was a quiet sort. We would walk behind the wagon for hours without him ever saying a word. I don't think he was bashful or unsure of himself. It was more that he simply did not engage in idle chatter. It about drove me crazy. I would ask a question or try and start a line of conversation and he would give me a one-word answer. Worse, sometimes he would not even acknowledge my question. By the time we settled in Eden, I knew we were not suited to one another.

"Max Loring often planned events to earn money for hymnbooks or other needed supplies for the community. I met Faron after a Sunday meeting, when Max had such an affair going. They drew names for a scavenger hunt and Faron and I ended up partners." She paused to look at him. Each regarded the other with a familiar look, one of mutual devotion. "It was magic between us, as if we were destined to be together."

"We did not hide anything," Faron was quick to point out. "I asked Laura if I could see her again and we began a courtship."

Laura continued. "Zeb came to me and demanded that I stop seeing Faron. I refused. I told him that I was not bound to him. In all of the discussions and throughout our journey, I never once agreed to marry Zeb. My traveling with them was no different than many others who came in the wagon train. There were a number of stragglers, people with no ties to anyone. I didn't feel that I should be forced into a marriage I didn't want."

"But Zeb didn't accept that," Jerrod observed.

"One night, after he had been drinking, he came to the ranch in a rage," Faron said, taking over the story. "When Laura refused to go with him, he called her a dirty name and shot her. If I hadn't shot back, he would have killed us both."

Jerrod was stunned. He looked at Laura in shock. "He shot you?"

At Faron's nod, she touched her right side. "The bullet tore a path along my ribs here."

"He tried to kill you!"

"He was going to kill us both," Faron confirmed. "The guy was out of his head. I didn't want a gunfight with him, Jerry. I never did a lot of practicing with a pistol, but when I heard Laura cry out, I knew I had to stop him. I fired back until my gun was empty." He shrugged. "Missed five of the six shots, but the one hit was square."

Laura took over again. "As luck would have it, Max Loring had gone hunting with Jake that very morning. Doreen was at our house. She bandaged my wound, and Max joined us in marriage that very evening. To prevent more bloodshed, we left the valley and came to Colorado."

"Did Stover know about this?"

Faron gave an offhand gesture. "Max knew how Stover felt about his brother. We loaded Zeb into Max's wagon, and he and Doreen took Zeb's body over to Stover's place. To spare the Gates family pain and humiliation, Max made out that the fight was simply between Zeb and me."

Laura wrung her hands. Her voice was full of guilt. "Even though there was never an actual promise between Zeb and me, there can be no doubt that Stover intended that we would marry one day. If he had demanded it before we left Ohio, I would have probably gone along with the marriage and been Zeb's wife. Stover was considerate enough to allow me to get to know his brother first. It turned out to be a mistake on his part, because I was not attracted to Zeb."

"No wonder he hates us," Jerrod said. "He was like a father to Zeb. I can see that he felt he had provided him a wife. Then the two of you get together and Zeb ends up dead."

Faron sighed. "Like I said, little brother, you've a hard road ahead. It would be a sight easier to drive a herd of wildcats with a wet noodle."

"I expect it will be a challenge."

"A challenge is understating the point, Jerry. Let me introduce you around. We've got some real fine gals hereabouts."

"I know what I want, Faron."

"It appears that you two are a lot alike," Laura said pointedly.

"Think maybe Jerry has the same good taste as I do?" Faron inquired with a smile at Laura.

Jerry experienced a rush of embarrassment as the two leaned toward each other and kissed. He felt his being there was an intrusion on their privacy. Still, it was the kind of marriage he wanted, one that was conceived out of love, not a mutual commitment or obligation brought on by two sets of parents. He was determined to settle for nothing less.

Max Loring stood before the farmers, a familiar figure, always strong in his faith, forever true in both his friendship and compassion. The dark circles under his eyes and underlying strain in his voice betrayed his usual confidence.

"It is our practice to pray on Sundays and praise God with song," he began. "However, we have some pressing matters that must be addressed today, before we commence with our usual meeting." His eyes swept over the crowd.

"Most of you have noticed there are a few missing among our number today. The Leinharts and Shultz families packed their belongings and have joined their relatives back east. The widow Morgan and her boys left last Monday. The Cragan family pulled out yesterday." His chest heaved with a sigh. "I blame none of these people for leaving the settlement. In fact"—he again ran his eyes over the group—"I would not blame anyone who packed up and left. This devastation will surely ruin a good many of us before next year's crop can be harvested."

"The hoppers are bound to be back next year, Max,"

one of the men said. "They surely left eggs behind. Come spring, there will likely be millions of hoppers to deal with again."

"Maybe those locusts were a sign from God," one man offered. "Could be that those people who pulled out were the smart ones. What if the Almighty don't want us settling out here? What if God wants us to return back east?"

"You can't believe a drought or bad winter means that God is angry with everyone living in that area!" Stover said vehemently. "Each of us is tested in life, but God is not in the habit of picking on a handful of people here or there. It is an act of Nature we have to face, the price of living on the plains."

The other man wilted under his domineering stare. He muttered, "Just thinking out loud."

"Besides, we will plan for them this round," Max vowed, stopping the discussion. "We can devise rolling crushers that will smash the hoppers as they appear. Several of us have worked together and built a model that should do the trick."

"What if they come back like this year?"

"That won't happen. They spread their eggs over several states and a few territories. We'll be able to kill them before they can mature. It will eliminate them from ever returning."

Andy Brown stood up. "So how do we survive until next year, Max? Most of us have lost everything we had. In a week or two, Toby and I will be without a bite of food in the house."

"Andy has a point," Stover put in. "Link Peters has closed the trading post for now. What he didn't lose to those hoppers, the rest of us have bought and taken home. He's cleaned out."

"Mayor Harker is lending Link some money to help reopen the store. He says they ought to have a shipment of food and supplies here in a few days."

Andy turned his head and spat into the dirt. "You know what that means, Max. We'll have to put up our deeds against the goods we charge. If the crops don't earn enough to pay the bills next season, either Link or Harker will foreclose on us. Between them, they'll own every homestead in the valley."

A good many grumbled their agreement. Max held up his hands to silence the group. When he had their attention, he produced a small black box.

"Here is the money we have collected for our school. I suggest that everyone contribute everything they have to spare."

"Why do we need a school now?" Andy Brown asked. "We'll all starve before it can be built."

"We won't use it for a school," Max replied. "We'll put it all together and order a winter store of supplies, to be shipped by rail as far as Ellis. We can send wagons to pick it up. With a bit of community effort, sharing, and the grace of God, we can make it through the winter."

"We don't have any cash," Andy said thoughtfully, "but we have a couple of mules we could sell."

"Yah!" Vernon spoke up. "I done got some pigs we sell, too."

"It would mean driving the stock to a buyer in Ellis or shipping them back east for higher prices."

A number of people began tossing around the idea of a major sale. Everyone offered to contribute. Before long, it was settled. Andy Brown was put in charge. He and three other men would transport their funds and all available livestock to Ellis. After selling the animals, they would make the order and await delivery of the goods. When they returned, Max would set up a fair system of distribution.

Marian, like most of the other women, remained silent throughout the meeting. Once the plan was accepted, Max turned to the usual Sunday service.

When the final "Amen" announced the end of the meeting, she hurried to the exit in an attempt to avoid Wolfgang. It was wasted effort, for he had been keeping sight of her. He caught up to her before she could reach the family wagon. He did not seem as cocksure of himself as usual. It had disturbed him, being outbid for her picnic basket.

"I been desire to ask your father for the courtship of you, Miss Marian," he said. "It is the way you asked, waiting for after the school charity."

"The arrival of those hoppers has put us in a rather poor state, Wolfgang. There is a great deal of work to do at the farm. I don't see how we would have any time for courtship."

"It be no problem. My father has already speak to Mr. Gates. We have permission." He was not to be put off.

Marian felt her heart sink in her chest. There was no escape. Her fate was sealed. She ducked her head, searching for the words that could dissuade Wolfgang. Her mind went blank.

He was quick to seize the advantage. "It be settled. Wednesday, I should come to visit. We will walk together and speak of our future."

Marian could not muster any words. Her throat was too constricted with emotion. Defeated and despondent, she could only manage a slight nod of her head.

"Ah-hah! Ah-hah!" Wolfgang laughed in triumph. "You see how good we be together, Miss Marian. You see!"

Tommy came up to her, even as Wolfgang was hurrying off to join his father. No words were necessary for him to recognize her misery.

"I overheard Vernon and Stover talking," he said quietly. "They have it all worked out for you. A Christmas engagement and a spring wedding."

She knotted her fists tightly and tears stung her eyes. "It isn't fair!" she blurted out. "Don't I have any choice about my future? Am I a horse to be bartered or sold?"

Tommy put a consoling hand on her shoulder. "I'm sorry, sis. I don't know how to stop it."

"I won't do it!" she insisted. "I don't care what it takes. I can't spend my life married to Wolfgang!"

"Might be a good idea not to speak out about it for a spell. Stover is still boiling mad over you ending up with Danmyer at the picnic. I think he is pushing this thing to prevent you from ever having a chance to see that rancher again."

"You notice that there was no Danmyer invited today."

Tommy shrugged. "They don't come to Sunday meetings. You know that."

"This was more than a religious gathering, Tom. They decided the fate of the valley without asking the Danmyers to be present."

"The mayor and a few others weren't there either. It don't mean nothing."

"You recall that after Faron killed Zeb, the Danmyers were shunned from most all the doings. Every time one of them showed his face, there was a fight. Vince Danmyer gave up even trying to court any of the girls in Eden. He met and married his Spanish wife while in Denver."

"So?"

"So the fight was between Faron and Zeb. Why should it involve the rest of the family? What's done is done!"

"Not exactly, sis. I heard Toby bragging about how he beat up one of the Mexican boys from the Danmyer ranch a while back. They're still considered outcasts."

"I wonder how much of that is envy?" she replied. "Their ranch is several times larger than what anyone else owns, plenty of water, a herd of cattle, the finest draft team for a hundred miles—I wonder if the hate directed at them is really because of Zeb Gates."

"Does it matter?"

Her shoulders sagged slightly. "I guess not. Stover would never accept Jerrod Danmyer courting me."

"Yeah. I believe his exact words at the picnic were that it would be over his dead body."

"What am I going to do, Tom?"

"I wish I knew, sis. I really wish I knew."

# CHAPTER 8

JAKE AND VINCE were there to greet Jerrod's return. He drove their wagon, while Reuben directed a team and wagon borrowed from Faron's ranch. Each pulled his team of horses to a stop, and Jake came around to the side of Jerrod's wagon.

"Glad to see you, son," he said. "We can sure use the grain you brought for the animals."

"Not to mention the other supplies," Vince put in, stepping around to join him. "You boys look beat."

"Been a dry haul," Jerrod explained. "Those hoppers didn't leave a blade of grass for the last hundred miles. How's the windmill holding up?"

"Still producing, and we had a pretty good rain a couple of days after you left. It washed a good portion of that hopper waste out of the country. The creek flooded in spots and is running clean enough for the animals to drink."

"What about the farmers?"

"Max Loring came by and asked if we could spare drinking water. We filled several barrels for him. He's the only one we've seen."

"How is everyone else holding up?"

"Max said the farmers got themselves a plan to make a trip to the railroad at Ellis and pick up enough supplies to get through the winter. A few have already pulled stakes."

"We fared better than most. Our herd reached Denver with only the loss of a few head."

"How's Faron?"

"Looking real good. The kids are growing like wild-flowers."

Jake smiled. "I'll maybe take his wagon back once we get things organized. Been a couple of years since I went to visit."

"Soon as we get this stuff unloaded, I'd like to take a ride."

A knowing look entered Jake's weathered face. "You won't take any advice about this gal?"

"Nope."

"You'll either get your heart busted or a bullet drilled through it."

"Guess that's the chance I'll have to take."

He grunted. "Headstrong whelp. Must be from your mother. I've always been a reasonable sort."

"Honest as the day is long, too," Jerrod quipped. "Would never think of exaggerating the truth a mite."

"Couldn't have said it better myself, son." He grinned. "Maria has been fixing tortillas today. I reckon you're about ready for a decent meal."

"Laura is a good cook, but it's been four days since we left Denver. I'm ready."

"Get yourself washed up. You can tell us all about Faron and his family over supper."

Jerrod gave a nod of his head, but the washing would wait. He and the others had to unload the two wagons first.

"Have any real trouble?" Vince asked, once Jake had gone into the house.

"On our return trip we happened onto a family about sixty miles out from Denver. Looked like they ran out of water and got lost. Seven souls, all of them dead."

"What a shame."

"Seen several more fresh graves along the way and a good many animals that had perished, too. I figure some of the critters got sick trying to drink the contaminated water or from eating hoppers."

Vince clenched his teeth. "They were a pestilence right out of the Bible."

"I reckon."

"They'll be back next year. Ain't no way they didn't lay eggs when they were here."

"We'll have to deal with them. Maybe with some poison grain, or we could bring in a few thousand chickens to eat them as they hatch."

"Their flavor taints any creature that eats them. Loring said that Kruger slaughtered a hog for food, but it tasted so bad they couldn't eat it. We had chicken for supper the other night and it was the same. It tasted like them wretched hoppers. Even milk from the cow has a distinct flavor."

"Once the animals get back on the grain we brought, it ought to clear up."

"Let's hope so. I like Mexican dishes, but not a steady diet."

"Beats going hungry," Jerrod said. "I wonder how the farmers are doing?"

"One family in particular, I imagine."

"Hate to see any of them starve."

"Yeah, it's going to be tough on a lot of them."

"Well, let's get this wagon unloaded. I don't want to have to ride too late after dark."

"Stover won't let you see his girl again."

"I'll slip by and see how they're doing. Might get a word with her, without getting myself shot."

"That will be a good trick, with Stover having a loaded gun at hand. You be careful, big brother. I mean it."

"That's always my intention, Vince."

Marian cringed when she heard the knock at the door. It was Wolfgang, a box of taffy in one hand and his hat in the other.

"Ah-hah," he greeted Stover. "I done come to see Miss Marian, Mr. Gates."

Her father turned around and regarded her with narrowed eyes. "You have a caller, Marian."

She did not hesitate, steeling herself with rigid determination. "Yes, sir," she answered, and hurried past Stover. She took the taffy, placed it on the chair nearest the door, then grabbed Wolfgang by the arm and propelled him back out the door. A few steps put them into the evening dusk.

"Where we going, Miss Marian?" Wolfgang asked, a wide grin of anticipation pasted on his thick lips. "Ah-hah! You taking me behind the barn or somewhere like that?"

"I need to speak to you in private," she replied.

"Sure! That be what I like, too. I am having to learn much about this courting game."

Marian led him around to the blind side of the house and walked until they reached the main trail. She had to be certain Stover could not eavesdrop on anything that passed between them.

When she stopped, Wolfgang automatically took her hand. She did not pull away, but rotated around to face him squarely. Viewing him objectively, she knew she would never be able to love him. He would be a good provider, as dependable as a hound dog and equally affectionate, but she was in love with Jerrod.

"I wish to discuss something with you, Wolfgang. It is very serious."

"Ah-hah! You can bet I'm thinking about the same thing!"

"No, I don't believe you are."

"What do you speak of, Miss Marian? Why do you bring me down to the road to talk?"

She took a deep breath and exhaled slowly. There was no easy way to say what she intended. It was brutal to be candid, but she had to make herself understood.

"I don't wish to hurt you, Wolfgang," she murmured, "but my heart belongs to another man."

Wolfgang's smirk and inane laughter disappeared at

once. He stared at her in disbelief, mouth agape. As it sank into his head that she was serious, he released her hand.

"I didn't wish for it to happen," she hurried forth. "It was an accident of fate."

"You say this to me?" he said incredulously. "You love someone else?"

"Yes, Wolfgang. I admire you too much to deceive you about it."

His head rolled from side to side, his eyes bugged in astonishment. It was as if the thought of being refused had never entered his mind.

"Besides that," she hurried on, "you should be free to court several girls. It should be your choice as to the girl you marry. Marriage should be something you decide on, not an arrangement your father negotiates."

"It is Danmyer, I bet. He bought your basket!"

"Does it really matter, Wolfgang? The most important thing is for you to tell your father and anyone else you like that I won't do. You deserve better, and you should have a number of girls to choose from. Why tie yourself down with me, when you are only now beginning to enter courting?"

"I been thinking of you for my wife, Miss Marian. It is not only my father that chose you."

"But don't you see, Wolfgang? You could never love me, knowing that I had given my heart to another man."

He thought about that. When he looked at her, she knew he'd made a decision. Even in the shadows of early night-fall, she could see the gleam in his eyes.

"You kissed Danmyer. Some of the others saw it."

She was immediately ashamed. "It was not something I planned. I didn't mean for it to happen."

"If you kissed him, you got to kiss me too!"

"What?"

"It is the only way to know who you really love. How are you so sure, if you have never kissed another man?"

"I told you, I didn't intend to kiss him."

Wolfgang stubbornly shook his head. "You kissed him. It is a fair test for you to kiss me too. I should have an equal chance."

Marian looked around quickly, an eerie feeling causing the hairs at the back of her neck to tingle, as if they were not alone. Wolfgang crowded her and put his hands on his hips.

"Well, Miss Marian? Do you give me kiss, or do we say to Mr. Gates about your decision?" A stern expression crossed his face. "If your father give your hand for me, you then have no choice. You will kiss me whenever I ask."

"Wolfgang, this is ridiculous."

"Not so," he said stubbornly. "It is only a fair test."

She took another deep breath and braced herself. "Very well, Wolfgang, but it will mean nothing to me."

His chest puffed up. "We have yet to see that."

Marian was rigid as Wolfgang came forward. His arms went around her, pulling her tightly against him. The lips that came to crush her own were filled with a desperate desire to overcome her resistance. She was uninspired by the kiss. It was the unwanted touch of his mouth against her own. She endured the endless moments, hating the humiliation, frantically wishing he would give up.

But Wolfgang was asserting his manhood, attempting to overwhelm her with his passion. It seemed his impotent embrace lasted an eternity. At the moment she decided he had been given ample time, there came the sound of an approaching horse.

"Standing in the road like that could get a person run over," said a cool, recognizable voice from the darkness.

To Marian's dismay, Jerrod was on Bingo, not fifty feet away! She struggled to free herself from Wolfgang, but he had his arms wrapped tightly about her and refused to release his hold.

"Don't let me interrupt," Jerrod spoke icily. "I was only passing by."

Marian pushed hard against Wolfgang's chest, forcing

him to let go. It was too late, as Jerrod had spun Bingo around and dug his heels into her ribs.

"Jerrod! Wait!" Marian cried.

But the horse responded at once, bolting up the dark trail. Marian raced after him and called out to his deaf ears. She ran down the trail until her legs ached and her lungs burned for want of air. Blinded by tears of shame and self-blame, she stumbled into a rut and went sprawling into a headlong slide.

Wolfgang came huffing and puffing up to where she was picking herself up. Rather than brush herself off, she wiped the tears from her eyes, smearing her cheeks with dust-covered hands.

"Miss Marian?" Wolfgang panted anxiously. "Are you injured?"

"I'm all right," she managed, looking in the direction of the distant rider. He was lost to the darkness. For a long time, she stared off into space, hoping against common sense that he would return.

"There be Danmyer, the one you think you love. See how he would not listen? You don't want him."

"I—I can't help the way I feel."

"He saw us kissing. He will not forget it."

"It was a mistake."

After a short pause, Wolfgang cleared his throat. "I am go home now, Miss Marian. You think of future, of becoming my wife. It is the right answer."

She did not reply as he whirled about and walked off toward the house and his waiting horse. It was only then that she gathered her senses enough to brush off the dust on her clothes.

*When and how will I ever get a chance to tell Jerrod what happened tonight?* If their places had been reversed, she knew the anger, hurt, and jealousy she would have felt at seeing him kiss another girl. Would she have given him a chance to explain?

*　　*　　*

Jerrod was not in the mood to return home. He took a wide turn and rode toward Eden. The only lights that shone were at a house or two and the tavern. He reined up at the hitching post in front of Keno's place and climbed down. Cynically, he thought how appropriate it was that the grasshoppers had not done much damage to the drinking establishment.

"Even hoppers have better sense than to consume rotgut whiskey," he muttered, tying up his horse.

Inside, two tables were occupied, a paint-faced woman was playing solitaire, and Toby Brown was standing at the bar, facing Keno. As Jerrod entered, Toby pivoted about, appraised him shortly, then purposely leaned over to spit into a brass spittoon at his feet. There was contempt in his action. It was similar to how a good many of the farmers behaved toward the Danmyer family. Ordinarily, Jerrod ignored the childish mannerisms. Tonight, he did not.

"Thought you went to Ellis, Toby," Jerrod said. "I wondered why the rotten smell hadn't cleared out of the valley."

Toby swung around and leaned both elbows on the counter. His hostile eyes measured Jerrod from head to foot. After a lengthy moment, he sneered and said, "This is a drinking parlor for men, Danmyer. You don't qualify to come in here."

"Seeing's how you are at the bar, Keno can't be too strict in his enforcement of that rule."

The muscles worked around Toby's thick-lipped mouth. Keno smiled, recognizing that the gauntlet had been tossed into the bully's face. All eyes in the room were on the two of them. It caused Toby to instill a belligerent challenge in his voice. "I used that Mexican pal of yours for a mop, Danmyer. If you know what's good for you, you'll get out of town."

"Maybe you'd care to step out and show me the way. I often get lost and confused in these big cities."

Toby straightened up, hitched his pants, and flexed his shoulders. He obviously enjoyed being the center of attention. Jerrod knew that a bully was nothing without a crowd. There were enough people present that Toby was spurred on.

"I'll show you how to eat dirt, Danmyer. I'm gonna shove your face into the biggest pile of horse leavings I can find."

"Now, there's a coincidence," Jerrod retorted with a smile. "You're the biggest pile of horse leavings I know of."

"Take it outside," Keno warned them both. "I don't allow no fighting in my place."

Toby's face grew dark. His hard glare made his eyes appear like mere slashes below his bushy eyebrows. He doubled his fists and stomped forward.

Jerrod held the door for him, until he was within a step, then he let it shut in his face. Toby threw open the door, as Jerrod backed out into the street.

"I'm gonna make you wish you'd never crossed me, Danmyer!"

"You going to breathe in my face?" Jerrod countered. "That would be taking an unfair advantage, Toby."

The man came off of the steps, his meaty paws raised. "We'll see how funny you are when I pound you into a puddle."

Jerrod was the taller of the two, but Toby had a fifty-pound advantage. He would be a bull, but Jerrod figured he was the quicker of the two.

Keno, the woman who worked for him, and the men followed from the bar. A couple of farmers began calling out, encouraging Toby. Keno grinned in anticipation, but offered no support to either one.

Toby immediately pressed forward, shooting out a right fist. Jerrod ducked away and also evaded the man's follow-up left jab. Several vicious, roundhouse swings got only air.

The bully grew frustrated. "Stand and fight, you yella—"

Jerrod launched a lightning right hand. It smacked Toby square in the mouth, cutting his sentence short and splitting his lip. He backed up a step and spat out both blood and his chaw of tobacco.

"Lucky punch, cowboy!" he muttered.

The two of them circled and exchanged blows, each trying to score a solid hit. Jerrod kept moving, always just out of reach. Toby put a lot of power in his wasted swings and was soon panting, laboring from the effort. He had also been drinking enough to slow his reactions. Jerrod began jabbing with his left hand, striking Toby in the face. The stinging shots were not hard enough to back him off, but it was constant punishment.

Toby slashed out with his fists and got only air. He charged wildly, but Jerrod was too quick on his feet, side-stepping and shoving the man right past his position. The harmless battle dragged out for several minutes. Toby was soon worn down from the exertion. He had lost his hat, sweat ran down his face, his lip was split, and blood seeped from his nose. He was gasping for air while Jerrod was still fresh.

Hesitation began to show in the brute's attempted swings; Toby was no longer confident of victory. He grew careful, while stubbornly seeking a weak spot in Jerrod's fighting style. The drink propelled him to continue the fight, but it was false courage. Within his eyes, Jerrod could see a glimmer of fear and uncertainty.

The cheering of the small crowd had waned. Most of them were smart enough to envision the eventual outcome. Toby was a brawler, while Jerrod was a shrewd fighter. Unless Toby landed a lucky punch, he was doomed.

Thinking of Paco, a man no more than half Toby's size, Jerrod grew serious and began to trounce his opponent. A quick jab to the man's right eye blinded Toby. Before he could clear his vision, Jerrod hammered him flush between the eyes. Toby's bulb nose cracked under the force. Even as he reeled from the solid shot, Jerrod pounded him about the ribs and drove a fist into his middle.

The assault staggered Toby. He backed away, trying to cover both his midsection and his face. The defense posture was not adequate protection to stop Jerrod's onslaught. He was suddenly enraged at Toby; he hated everything about him. He turned loose his fury and clubbed the man with rock-hard knuckles until the bully's strength gave way. A jolt to Toby's jaw sent him to his knees. He rocked there, eyes glazed, mouth wide open, arms hanging uselessly at his sides, unable to defend himself.

Jerrod drew back his fist, ready to smash Toby's ugly mug into a bloodied mass. The silence of the crowd told Jerrod he had won the fight. He hesitated, envisioning Marian kissing another man. It startled him, the realization that he had been venting his rage over witnessing her embrace.

Instead of finishing the man with a final brutal stroke to his exposed face, Jerrod left him teetering on his knees and walked over to the watering trough. He rinsed the blood off his knuckles, splashed water onto his face, and mounted his horse. A glance back over his shoulder allowed him to see two men hauling the unconscious Toby over to the same trough.

There was no sense of victory. Toby had beaten Paco only because he worked on the Danmyer ranch. He had thrown his weight around for years, usually picking on men smaller than himself. It was high time that someone trimmed his branches. But Jerrod realized that he had used those things as an excuse. Seeing Marian in another man's arms, he had been so filled with vehemence that he wanted to strike out at someone. Toby had been handy.

*What was she doing kissing another man? She seemed so sincere at the picnic. I would have bet my life that she had feelings for me!*

"You're a female, Bingo," he spoke to his horse. "Can you tell me why Marian would let another man kiss her?"

The horse perked her ears at hearing her name, but she did not reply to his question.

"I get it," Jerrod complained. "You won't tell me, because you females stick together." He grunted. "Remember that, when I accidentally forget to give you any oats tonight."

# CHAPTER 9

WHEN THE RIDER entered the yard, Marian stopped her scrubbing of Stover's shirt. She brushed at a pesky strand of hair that refused to stay pinned into place.

"It's Mr. Loring," Wilma said, looking out the window. "He has a solemn look about him."

Marian wiped her hands on her apron and followed her mother out onto the porch.

"Good day to you, Mr. Loring," Wilma greeted. "What brings you way out here?"

Max shifted his weight uncomfortably. "Is Stover about?"

"He and the boys took the wagon and went to gather cow chips. Need to put in a store for winter."

Max nodded. "Be back anytime soon?"

"We don't expect Mr. Gates until around dark. He and the boys usually make a full day of it." She smiled. "Since the hoppers swept the earth clean we now have to travel a long way to find any usable chips."

"No buffalo left anymore, either," Max agreed. "I imagine you have to cross onto Danmyer range to find fodder for your fire."

"Yes, but even that is no longer a sure thing. They moved most of their herd to Colorado."

Marian could see worry embedded in the man's face, sorrow in his eyes. Max was too caring a man to adequately hide his feelings. She felt an ominous sense about his coming to see them.

"What is it, Mr. Loring?" she asked, stepping up next to

102

her mother. "You came to tell us something. Is it bad news?"

Max frowned for a moment, then he relaxed and gave his head an affirmative nod. "I never was much good at hiding the truth."

"What truth?" Wilma asked.

"Andy Brown and the others were attacked on their return from Ellis. Andy was killed and another two were wounded." He swallowed against the emotion that flooded his voice. "The bandits stole their horses, wagons, and everything they were hauling. All of our money and sacrifice was for naught. The supplies are gone."

An emptiness invaded Marian's chest. Like all of the other farmers, they had been counting on a share of the food and grain that was being transported. Without it, the future was suddenly dark and uncertain.

"Poor Mr. Brown," Wilma said. "Is there any way of knowing who the attackers were?"

"Three or four masked men is all we know. Keno Dean took several men and went to look for them, but the bandits had a two-day head start. I don't expect a posse to find anything."

"What are we going to do, Mr. Loring? How can everyone survive without those provisions?"

"Mayor Harper has vowed to try and borrow money so he can extend credit until next harvest. Link Peters is presently in Denver, buying what supplies he can afford. I'm sure he will also grant credit to the citizens of Eden."

"They will both insist on a debt against our deed to our farms," Wilma said. "They would have to, in order to protect their own investments."

"That only makes sense, as they have their own business to think of. Regardless, I'm sure they will treat everyone fairly."

"Mr. Gates is not willing to borrow against our land," she

replied. "I don't know what we will do, but Stover has often said he would not put the farm in debt."

Max's face was drawn, his eyes full of sadness. "I wish I had some better news, Mrs. Gates. Tell Stover that we'll discuss our options at the Sunday meeting."

"I'll tell him."

Max tipped his head toward Marian. "Good day to you, ladies. I hope to see all of you this Sunday."

As he rode out of the yard, Wilma put a hand above her breasts and whispered, "Dear Lord, what are we to do?"

"We can't possibly make it till next harvest," Marian said.

"I know, dear. Even stretching everything we have, we will be lucky to get by until Christmas."

"What do you think Stover will do?"

Wilma ducked her head. "I don't know."

"Maybe Keno will find the bandits. He is supposed to be tough and experienced. There's a chance he will catch them."

"Poor Toby. He will be lost without his father. They were very close."

"Bet he sells the place to either Mr. Harker or Mr. Peters and is gone within a week."

Wilma sighed. "Let's get back to work. I'll speak to Mr. Gates as soon as he and the boys return. I'm sure he will figure something out."

Jerrod was picking through his clothes, packing a war bag for his upcoming trip, when Vince entered his room.

"Don't forget to pack your shaving kit, big brother. If I know Faron, he'll want to introduce you to every single girl that lives within a hundred miles. He had Maria and me paired off before I had time to remove my boots."

"Yeah, I've got my straight razor."

Vince frowned. "You don't sound very happy."

"It's a long ride, that's all."

"You hear the news about Andy Brown?"

"Pa told me at supper last night. Anything new?"

"Talked to Max Loring while I was picking up a replacement harness for the team. He said the posse spent a full day on the trail of the bandits, only to find the wagons at the edge of Raccoon Creek. They had been burned to ashes and the horse tracks went into the stream. They never could find where the bandits came out."

"Keno always bragged about being part hound dog— guess he was talking about his homely mug."

"No telling where all the supplies went. They might have had a wagon ready at the main road. With all the travelers that use the trail, they might have hauled the goods right back to Ellis."

"That makes sense. They couldn't have hauled the supplies down the creek on horseback."

"I guess spirits are pretty low around Eden. Max figures most will have to borrow from Harker or Link Peters to survive."

"Plays right into their hands, doesn't it? They were looking to earn commission on some land deals. Now they'll have a chance to foreclose on every place in the valley."

"Got to think like a husband and father, Jerry. What else can they do?"

"I expect Harker or Link bought out those German farmers who already pulled freight. They went back to Ohio to start over. I imagine they can resell those places for enough money to hang on till next harvest. Then the farmers who can't pay back their loans could be foreclosed on. Not much of a future here for most of them."

"Pa said there was quite a buzz about the beating you gave Toby. The gossip around town is that he never hit you once."

"Those people should have been me the next morning. I ached from head to foot."

"Well, he didn't mess up your face"—he simpered—"or so anyone would notice. With a puss like yours, it's tough to tell if you've been fighting or not."

"I love you, too, little brother."

"You don't have to go to Denver, you know. Pa said that the Sanchez boys could manage it on their own."

"That would put an unfair burden on Faron. He would have to oversee every aspect of the herd. I'll make the imposition as slight as possible."

Vince grinned. "The imposition? When did you start spouting such big words?"

"Read it in a book," Jerrod replied. "If you had learned to read, you could talk real educated too."

"I'd rather be the handsome one of the family. You go be the smart one."

Jerrod felt a pang. "Smart," he repeated. "I don't think I even understand the word."

"Something you want to talk about?"

"No," he said, thinking of how he couldn't leave without seeing Marian again. Arguably, it made good sense. If she said there was nothing between them, at least he could start looking at other girls. He hated the thought of a rejection from Marian, but he had to see her. Somehow, he had to find out the truth.

"Anything you need for the trip?"

Jerrod reached a decision. "I'm fine, Vince, but there's something I have to do. I might be late for supper."

"Maria can set aside a plate and some leftovers."

Saying a quick thanks, Jerrod went out and saddled Bingo. Within a few minutes, he was on the trail toward the creek. Stover would not let him see Marian, so he would have to find a back door.

As he rode, he wondered about the attack on the wagons. Every person in town had put money into that venture—all except for the three businessmen. In essence, Harker and Link could profit most from the loss of the supplies. With that hope gone, the people of Eden would be forced to go into debt to the bank and store.

But would Link or Harker resort to killing? he wondered. There was a strange fire earlier at the Brown place, too. Was all of this tied to someone wanting to kill Andy Brown?

If he had been going to stick around, he would have done some snooping on his own. As he was headed out of the state, there was little he could do. Max Loring was a capable man. He had been the town leader for ten years. If anyone could pull the farmers through this, he was the one for the job.

The ground was too level to approach the Gates house on the main trail, but there was a stretch of ground between the Gates property and the Brown place that could conceal his approach. It was a runoff ditch of sorts, a brush-laden wash that separated the boundaries of the two properties. By swinging wide and then moving slowly along the wash, Jerrod was able to ride to within a couple hundred yards of the sod house.

Once he had gotten as close as possible, Jerrod picketed Bingo where she would be out of sight. The brush was nothing but a few sticks. All of the leaves had been consumed by the hoppers. However, there were a few blades of grass that had pushed through since then. It gave Bingo something to nibble at.

Ducking low, Jerrod eased up to a runoff trench and lay belly-down behind a lone tumbleweed. He was able to see both the front of the house and the rear yard from his position.

After a few minutes of watching, he deduced that Stover and the boys were working on a fence. They were in sight, but a fair distance from the house. He could approach the house unseen, but there was Mrs. Gates to account for. Jerrod was uncertain of the reception he was going to get from Marian, let alone how her mother might react.

Even as he tried to figure a way to lure Marian outside or get her alone, Mrs. Gates appeared. She had a pitcher of something and several glasses on a tray. With a deliberate pace, she set off toward where the men were working.

*Yes, ma'am. That's what those fellows need, a cool drink and a few minutes to relax.* Even as he started to move, he anticipated that the woman would probably wait for them to drink the pitcher dry, then bring the dishes back with her. It was logical and would give him more time.

Rising up, he hurried along a course that was parallel to the house until it stood between him and the people working on the fence. Hidden from their view, he turned and jogged right toward the sod house. He risked being seen by anyone looking out the window on that side, but he had to take that chance. He was determined to speak to Marian. If she brushed him off like so much dust from her collar, he would know that he had only imagined her response during their kiss.

He slowed to a walk and padded over to peer into the window. It was a bedroom—Stover and Wilma's, from the looks of it. That meant his approach had been undetected.

Walking softly, he edged around the corner of the house and slipped quietly through the open door. Marian had her back to him, standing at the stove. She was using a heavy iron to press a pair of pants. He opened his mouth to speak, but was afraid she might cry out. It wouldn't do to have Stover and the boys come running to her aid.

Jerrod crept across the hardpack dirt floor to her. When she placed the iron on the stove to heat, he lurched forward, wrapping one arm around her to pin her arms and clamping his free hand over her mouth.

"Sh-h-h!" he began . . .

Marian's reaction was immediate. She threw her weight back against him and twisted in his grasp. As he sought to control her and gain his balance, her foot stomped down on his instep.

"Ye-ow!" he exclaimed, trying to maintain his hold.

About then, she got her mouth open and bit down on the callused flesh between his thumb and first finger. He jerked back, trying to release his hold. Too late!

Marian grabbed at the object on the stove and rotated with the speed of a cat. She wielded the heated iron, ready to smooth out every wrinkle in his face!

"Whoa!" he clamored, holding his hands out toward her. "Uncle! I give up! I surrender! Hold back your team!"

The expression on her face changed as quickly as her reaction. She stopped in midmotion, the iron held up as a weapon. Her eyes grew wide with wonder and she shook her head in disbelief.

"Jerrod?" she murmured. Then, with renewed ire, "Jerrod Danmyer! I ought to brand you with this iron for scaring me to death!"

Jerrod looked at the spot where his hand was beginning to bleed and hobbled over on his one good foot to sit on a stool. "You already branded me," he complained. "Talk about a tiger in a whirlwind. I pity the Indian who sneaks up on you."

Marian cast a worried glance out the door. "Mother will be back any minute. You must be crazy to come here."

Removing a dirty rag from his pocket, Jerrod began to dab at his injured hand.

"Not with that dirty thing," Marian scolded him. "I've got some water."

Jerrod sat quietly while Marian produced a pan of water and a strip of cloth. She dabbed at the hand a few minutes and it stopped bleeding.

"It isn't all that bad."

"You've got teeth like a wolverine."

"Serves you right, sneaking up on me like that."

"I was afraid you might scream."

"I'm not in the habit of screaming."

"Yeah, I noticed."

She raised her gaze to look at him and he was instantly lost in the liquid pools of her hazel eyes.

"Why are you here?"

Jerrod rallied his brain to function and let out a deep breath. "I'm leaving for Denver. I didn't know if it mattered to you or not, but I thought I'd tell you in person."

"Denver?" she whispered hoarsely.

"I have to tend the herd through the winter."

She ducked her head, lowering her eyes to hide her feelings. When she spoke, her words were carefully guarded. "Then I won't see you again."

"I'll probably come home for Christmas. It depends on the weather. Man wouldn't last long in a blizzard out on those open plains."

"I suppose not."

"Will you be here?"

Marian hesitated before answering. "Stover is a very determined man. He won't give up our farm without a fight."

"I heard about the supplies being lost. Also that Andy Brown was killed."

"And I understand you gave Toby the beating of his life."

Jerrod winced at the memory. "I was in a bad mood."

"It was the same night you . . ." she seemed to back up a step, as if she had to take a run at what she wanted to say, "the night you rode past here."

"Yeah."

"What you saw," she began softly, "what you think you saw," she corrected hurriedly, "was not as it might have appeared."

"It doesn't matter."

Her head snapped up. "What do you mean—it doesn't matter!"

"I've had time to think over what happened at the picnic. I expect you were only feeling indebted to me for spending twenty dollars for your basket and company."

Immediately, Jerrod knew he had stuck his foot into a

bear trap. A dark fury swept Marian's face. There was a blur before his eyes and a hand smacked him soundly across the cheek. It was forceful enough that it nearly unseated him.

"How dare you say something like that to me! What kind of girl do you think I am?"

"I only thought that—"

"I'll tell you what I'm not, Mr. Danmyer!" She curtly stopped his lame explanation, glowering at him, until he backed off of the stool for the safety of added distance. "I'm not for sale—not for twenty dollars! Not for a thousand times that!"

"I didn't mean—"

She once more silenced his excuse, her voice rising with her ire. "Just because you saw Wolfgang kissing me, that doesn't mean that I let anyone kiss me. I was forced to allow him that liberty to convince him that I didn't love him—okay?" She was shouting now. "I know it sounds stupid, but I had to operate on his level! In fact," she was practically screaming, "I'm beginning to think that all men are stupid! Blind, dumb, and stupid!"

"Marian!" a voice called from outside the house. "You all right in there?"

The rage left instantly. "Stover! He must have heard us!"

"Us?" Jerrod was indignant. "You're the one doing the screaming."

Marian hurried over to look out the front door. "Stover is coming this way!" she whispered fearfully. "You've got to get out of here!"

"I'll speak to him."

"He won't take time to listen, and I don't want the two of you fighting." She was adamant. "Get out of here—now!"

"But he heard you yelling. He is bound to—"

Marian sprang to the stove, grabbed up the hot iron, and touched it to the back of her hand. She sucked in her breath as it immediately burned the flesh.

"Through the window in the bedroom!" she directed. "Go!"

Jerrod gave her a single look—a sorry substitute for everything he had wanted to say—then darted into the side room. He went out the window and was easing it closed as he heard Stover's booming voice from inside.

"What's the trouble, gal! What's going on?"

"I'm sorry, sir," Marian whimpered softly. "I got careless and burned my hand. I was venting my wrath over being such a dolt."

"Let's have a look." Stover sounded concerned.

Those were the last words Jerrod overheard, breaking away in a straight line from the house. Once even with the wash, Jerrod ran low to the ground. He managed to reach Bingo without being seen and went back the way he had come.

Thirty minutes later, after crossing the creek, he was able to breathe normally again. He had been successful in his attempt to see Marian, but it was disturbing that he had not accomplished much of anything.

*Well, I did learn a couple things.* He had to smile. *I learned never to sneak up on that gal, unless I want my skull caved in, and I also unearthed that she was forced into kissing that Wolfgang character.*

He tried to remember Marian's every word. How had she put it? She had kissed the fellow to show him that she did not love him. Was that a strange logic or what?

"Bingo," he began, "are you quite sure that you won't . . ." He saw the way she perked her ears at the sound of her name. "Never mind," he said, "even if you could talk, I doubt you'd give me a straight answer."

# CHAPTER 10

THE SNOW WAS only two or three inches deep, except for an occasional drift, windswept, crusted over from the icy temperature. The sun produced a blinding glare and made it extremely difficult to find any buried cow chips.

"We've been over this area before," Tommy complained. "The only place to find chips is to go farther onto Danmyer range."

"Stover would tack our hides to the woodshed."

Tommy adjusted the cloth that was wrapped around his ears. With his hat pulled on tight and his coat collar turned up, all that showed of his face was his nose and eyes.

Marian was bundled up as well, wearing her warmest dress, Stover's heavy coat, and three pair of socks inside his old shoes. She reasoned that the two of them must look like the kind of beggars who live in the back alleys of a big city, or hermits who shun contact with other people and sleep in caves.

The wind whistled into her face and she ducked her head against the tiny crystals of blowing snow. The chill penetrated into her bones.

"Is Wolfgang coming over again Saturday night?"

"He seems determined. The more I try and discourage him, the more he keeps coming back."

"At least you've been over to Sunday dinner a couple times. Bet they set a better table than we do."

"Can't argue there. Mrs. Kruger always has plenty on the table to eat. I wish there was some way to bring some of it back home."

"Maybe you ought to rethink your stance about tying the

marriage knot with Wolfgang. You wouldn't go hungry or freeze."

"I can think of worse things than being hungry or cold, Tom. Would you enjoy listening to that 'Ah-hah! Ah-hah!' for the rest of your life?"

He groaned. "He does test the nerves on occasion."

"Besides, I don't have any affection for him. I wish I did. I wish he was the kind of man I could love and cherish, but he's not."

Tom kicked a hard lump, but it was only a dirt clod. "This is useless," he whined. "We're going to be out here all day and get nothing for our trouble."

"We have to find some fuel. We'll all be done like Brandon if we don't get something for the fire."

"I don't care what Stover says," Tommy said. "Brandon ain't going to get better unless we heat the house. His cough is getting worse every day."

Marian looked back toward their farm. They had already crossed the creek onto Danmyer range. She was equally concerned over the health of her brother. Everyone in the family had developed colds from inadequate heating and lack of proper food. They would soon be mere skeletons, and less meat on the bones meant being more affected by the cold.

"All right, Tom. Where do you want to look?"

"I've seen a few head of cattle over east of here. It's where the Danmyers have been wintering the cattle that weren't driven to Denver. I'll bet there are enough chips there to fill our bags in a matter of minutes."

Marian walked over to their horse. She mounted first and put her leg forward to allow Tommy to step into the stirrup and swing up behind. "If Stover finds out, this was your idea," she warned.

"Let's hurry," Tommy replied. "I've about lost feeling in my hands and toes."

"Mine have been numb for the past hour."

The shaggy plow horse moved at a slow pace, also weak

from lack of decent food. When it came onto a sad-looking sagebrush, it ducked its head and snatched a mouthful of scraggly branches. Continuing, the horse turned its head slightly to one side and then the other, trying to get the tough fodder in a position for chewing.

They continued for twenty minutes before they reached the bare pasture. "There!" Tommy pointed past her shoulder. "I told you!"

Marian blinked her watering eyes against the dazzle of the sun. There were numerous roundish lumps scattered about under the snow.

"I see them!" she exclaimed. "Let's hurry this up."

They tied the horse to another sparse sagebrush, where she could nibble at the skeletal branches, and grabbed their gunnysacks.

It was like Christmas, running from one frozen chip to another. A kick or two loosened the chip from the ground. Quickly, the snow was brushed off, and it was tossed into the sack. In a matter of minutes, they had filled both sacks.

"Stover is going to want to know how we came by so many chips," Marian warned. "We better come up with a good story."

"How about we tell him we followed the creek and found where some cattle had been coming for water?"

"He won't believe it. You know he—" Marian stopped, shocked to see a rider moving toward them. "Tommy!" she whispered. "Someone's coming."

There was no chance to run. They were a good fifty yards away from their horse. As the man drew closer, Marian recognized Vince Danmyer.

"Howdy, kids!" he greeted. "Picking up chips?"

"I . . . that is, we . . ." Marian cleared her throat. "We didn't mean to trespass onto your land, Mr. Danmyer. It's only that the chips are mostly gone from our side of the creek."

Vince stopped a few feet away and looked them over. A smile came to his lips. "You're Marian Gates."

"Yes."

He chuckled. "I about didn't recognize you under all those clothes. You look half frozen."

"It is cold today."

"Need some help?"

"No. Our bags are full. We were about to leave."

Vince waved an arm. "Anytime you want—there's a fair amount of fodder for the fire in this pasture. We only kept a few head of cattle here on the place. I guess I don't have to tell you that those hoppers ate most of the grass down to the roots."

"Our place too."

"How is the family?"

"We're getting by."

Vince took a closer look at her. "I don't know if it means anything to you or not, but Jerry is coming for a visit in a few days. I imagine he'll bring some supplies from Denver. Maybe you and your family would like to come over for Christmas dinner?"

She was surprised by his offer. Nothing would have pleased her more than to accept. However, that was impossible.

"Mr. Gates still holds a grudge against your family for the death of my uncle. I'm sure he would refuse."

"Too bad about that," Vince said. "You are actually our closest neighbors. Be nice if we were on friendly terms with one another."

"I agree, but Stover is not a forgiving man."

"We have a store of coal for our stoves, so feel free to come pick up all the chips you want," Vince offered.

"That's very decent of you."

"Be seeing you."

They watched Vince turn his horse and ride away. Tommy let out the breath he had been holding. "I thought we'd had it there."

"I keep telling you, the Danmyers are not a bunch of cold-blooded killers. Jerrod told me that Zeb was drunk when he went to the Danmyer ranch. He started shooting first. Faron only returned fire."

"Stover still blames Faron for stealing Laura away from Zeb. He says the kidnapping was what caused Zeb to go out to the ranch. He was trying to get Laura back."

"If that were the complete truth, why didn't the entire valley go out with him? Kidnapping is against the law. Also, why would Laura marry Faron? I mean, would you marry someone who kidnapped you and killed the one you were promised to?"

Tommy grinned. "I don't know. You think some wild woman might kidnap me one day?"

"Forget I asked you the question."

A gust of wind swirled the snow about their faces. It was a grim reminder of why they were standing out on the frozen ground.

"Let's get home, Tom. My hands and feet are blocks of ice."

"You don't have to tell me twice. I believe my ears fell off about an hour ago. Think we can paste them back on?"

Marian did not reply. She lifted her sack and hurried toward the horse. Even as her teeth were chattering from the chill of the cold, she was warmed at one thought. Jerrod was coming home for a visit. With a great deal of luck, he would figure a way to see her. She didn't know how he would manage such a feat, but she was sure he would try.

Jerrod stood in front of the potbellied stove and flexed his numb fingers. They were beginning to sting from being warmed. The pressure built until his hands felt ready to explode, so he moved back a little and waited for the pain to subside.

"Fool stunt, son." Jake shook his head. "You might have died out on the prairie coming here in this kind of weather."

"I put up a shelter and carried a little wood for a fire. My main concern was that Bingo might freeze. Had to keep the pace slow enough that she didn't work up a lather."

"Paco is rubbing her down at the barn. Lots of warm straw and a good helping of oats, she ought to be all right."

"How about things around here? What's been happening?"

"Ran into Max Loring the other day. He says that Toby Brown pulled stakes and left the valley."

"Toby did?" Jerrod shook his head in wonder. "He was one that I figured would never sell. Bully that he was, he and his dad could raise a beautiful crop."

"With Andy gone, maybe he didn't have the heart for farming."

"How much do you think his place brought?"

"No one seems to know. Toby just packed up and left without a word to anyone."

"Their place was good land. I'll bet his deed is picked up by some of those folks back east. But after the bout with those hoppers this year, I don't think I'd be in any hurry to buy a farm here in Eden."

"The German family south of the Kruger place also packed up and left. The woman was down sick, and two of their six kids had died from hunger and the cold. I believe Harker gave them a few dollars for their deed. All their years of work was for naught."

"Guess about everyone owes Harker money?"

"Either him or Link or both."

Vince came into the room. He had two steaming cups of coffee. "This ought to warm your innards."

Jerrod took the coffee and allowed the heat from the cup to soothe the ache in his fingers. He could move all of his toes, and the grayish tint about his face had disappeared. There was no indication of frostbite, but he had been very close.

"Max said the cold and lack of supplies is taking a heavy toll," Jake continued. "There has been no less than a dozen deaths from either freezing to death or hunger. Out of three newborns in the past four months, two didn't make it."

"It's a sorry situation," Vince agreed. "Most have borrowed from Harker and run up a big tab at Link Peters's store. The choice is to either end up deep in debt or wind up starving and dying from the cold. I ain't seen a smile since winter set in."

"Wonder how Link is staying in business? Think he has taken a loan out of the bank, too?"

"Probably," Jake replied. "I'd say both he and Harker must have floated some kind of loan from those potential buyers."

"Anything on the bandits who killed Andy Brown?"

"Nothing."

"I can't believe Toby would up and leave while his father's killer is still running loose."

"Cut his losses and got out," Vince suggested. "Guess he wasn't as bullheaded as we thought."

"What about help from the government? Anything being done to help the starving farmers?"

"Those hoppers cut a swath from the Dakotas to Texas. People have packed up and moved or died from the cold and starvation all along their route. Far as we've heard, nothing is in the works for any of them."

"There won't be any notice for the plight of the farmers until the people back east get hungry."

"I reckon."

Jerrod sat down and sipped at the hot liquid. "Sure am glad I made the trip. You guys are full of good news."

"I did happen onto your gal a while back," Vince informed him. "She and her brother were down in the east pasture picking up cow chips."

"How'd she look?"

"Like a beggar in rags, Jerry. She was so bundled up, I wasn't sure she was even a gal for a bit."

"They doing all right?"

"I don't know. Stover is a headstrong sort. I'll bet he isn't of a mind to crawl to Harker for credit."

"They have to eat."

"I couldn't see them for all the clothing, but both kids looked a little gaunt about the face. I expect they're making do with a handful of beans each week."

"You know those kids were desperate for heating fuel if they came all the way out to our east pasture. Stover would never approve of their coming that far onto our property."

"How are you ever going to win the girl's hand?" Vince asked.

Jake joined in. "Stover won't ever agree to let you court his daughter, son. I was hoping that Faron would introduce you to some gals around Denver."

"He tried, but I've made up my mind."

"How can you make up something you have so little of?" Vince quipped.

"If I want to know your opinion, little brother, I'll ask Maria to give it to me."

"Speaking of Maria," Jake jumped in to stop the bantering, "I'll bet she has dinner on the table. Why don't you two wash up, while I check on it?"

As their father left the room, Vince grew deadly serious. "It ain't good, Jerry. There are people dying of hunger all around us."

"What can we do about it?"

"We were hurt by those hoppers, too. Buying and transporting grain and supplies from Denver to feed the stock we kept here on the ranch has us scratching for pennies. If we should have a bad spring and lose a number of calves, we might end up working for wages at some other ranch."

"Faron had to pay out good money to graze our herd, too. It didn't help his situation, as he is in debt with his own place."

"Even so, we are a thousand times better off than some of these farmers. I spoke to Max about it, and he said some of them are shooting magpies for food or boiling old hides for soup. They can't hold on much longer."

"I'll ride by and speak to Max. There must be something we can do."

"Reckon I know the route you'll take into town." He winked. "Maria might fix up some tortillas and cornbread for Max and the Gates family—kind of a Christmas gesture, if you get my drift?"

"Thanks, Vince. I'd appreciate it."

"Then I'll make arrangements for your funeral," he said, grinning. "After all, what are brothers for?"

"I've asked myself that a number of times, Vince. I really have."

The sound of a rider sent Marian scurrying to the window. She lifted the corner of the cardboard covering and peeked out. The figure sitting atop a horse was one she quickly recognized.

Stover opened the door a crack and glared out at Jerrod. "You ain't welcome here, Danmyer!" he snarled.

"Don't get your back arched like a spooked cat, Stover. I'm only here as a favor to Max Loring. He sent this basket for you, said it was a season's greeting to your family."

"Max? He sent us a basket?"

"I'd admire to warm up a bit before heading on back to the ranch. The wind today is cold enough to put frost on the devil's windows."

"Five minutes," Stover allowed. "But it don't mean we are going to start sitting together at the Sunday meeting."

Jerrod swung down and removed a basket from behind the saddle. Marian quickly fluffed her hair with both hands and pinched her cheeks for color. When Jerrod entered the room, he stopped, allowing his eyes to adjust to the darkness.

"There be the stove to warm yourself," Stover told him. "I've got my timepiece handy."

Jerrod stepped over and placed the basket on the table. He paused to smile at Wilma and removed his hat.

"Appreciate the hospitality, ma'am."

"You say Mr. Loring sent us the basket?"

"Yes, ma'am. I ran into him this morning and offered to save him the ride."

Marian subtly moved over, as if to examine the contents of the basket. She was wary of Stover's watchful eye. Carefully, shē lifted the top and began to remove the parcels of food.

"Cornbread, tortillas, potato cakes, and"—she picked up a round item and lifted it to her nose—"apple pie!"

"Wow!" Tommy clamored. "Where do you suppose Max got any apples?"

"Sounds great!" Brandon said hoarsely, rising up from a bed by the fire.

Marian raised a look into Jerrod's eyes. She already knew the truth of the matter: to her knowledge, Mrs. Loring had never prepared tortillas.

"You folks making out all right?" Jerrod asked, turning the attention away from the food.

"We got no complaints," Stover replied. "You can see that we're all accounted for."

"Those hoppers didn't leave much behind."

"They didn't get our potato crop, except to eat the tops off of the plants. We'll still be here come spring."

"Glad to hear it."

"I'll wager you are," Stover said sourly.

Jerrod rotated to face him. "You sure are the sort to hold a grudge."

"A man what's dead stays that way a long time, Danmyer."

"I had nothing to do with your brother and Faron, Mr. Gates. I was off fighting in the war when all of that took place."

"Blood is the same. You're a Danmyer."

"I reckon you don't listen much to those Sunday meetings of yours, Stover. What about all that 'Love thine enemy' and 'Forgive those what done trespass against you'? Those just so many words to you?"

"I adhere more to "An eye for an eye' and 'Thou shalt not kill,' Danmyer."

He sighed. "I'd admire to be friends, Stover."

"I done seen the friendship you have—for my daughter."

"Won't argue that point, sir. It would be a privilege to come courting."

"Not so long as I draw a breath of air."

Jerrod chuckled at the vehemence in his voice. "I can see you haven't yet made up your mind for certain."

Stover did not find humor in his words. "The clock is ticking. Two more minutes."

"Dag'gum, Stover, we're neighbors. We should be helping one another."

"Your family murdered my brother, Danmyer. Don't ever ask to come into my house again."

Jerrod stared at Stover for a long minute, the meeting of two strong wills, a silent battle of strength. Stover was first to look away—only to check his watch.

"Time's up, Danmyer. Ride on."

"Thank you for bringing the basket," Mrs. Gates murmured.

Marian could see that her mother knew the truth of its origin. When Jerrod looked in Marian's direction, she dared not speak. It was risking a tongue-lashing to even make eye contact.

"So long, mud kitten," he said, showing a half-smile. Then he went past Stover and out the door. When he put his horse into motion, it was not in the direction of the Danmyer ranch.

Stover had to have noticed him heading toward town, but he kept his thoughts to himself. He was aware of the joyful anticipation in the eyes of his family over the food basket. Jerrod had said the meal came from the Lorings. That allowed him to accept the food without shame.

"Looks as if we'll have a Christmas dinner after all!" Brandon said. "I can't wait!"

Tommy chimed in, "Sure be a change of pace from our beans-and-gruel diet."

Wilma smiled at his enthusiasm. "Give me a minute to heat things up a little and fix some tea."

Marian felt a churning inside. It was not only hunger for food. Seeing Jerrod again, she knew it was also the flutter of her uncontrollable heart.

"Nice of Danmyer to bring the basket all the way out here," Tommy observed. "Too bad we have to be enemies."

Stover glowered a warning. "He killed your uncle Zeb, son."

"Faron killed Zeb," Tommy corrected him carefully. "It was a fight between the two of them. Like Jerrod said, he was off fighting in the war at the time."

"A man is responsible for the actions of his kin. Zeb was my brother. His kin killed him in cold blood."

"It was a gunfight, sir. Zeb went to the Danmyer ranch. He could as easily have killed Faron."

"That's enough!" Stover told him firmly. "We ain't going to talk about a Danmyer in this house. You understand me?"

"Yes, sir." Tommy gave ground. "I was only voicing my opinion."

Marian felt a warmth enter her being. Her brother had taken up for Jerrod against her father. He was quickly becoming a man.

"This all looks and smells delicious," Wilma interrupted, spreading out plates on the table. "Come and get it."

# CHAPTER 11

MAX FROWNED. "I can't tell an outright lie, Jerrod. If Stover should confront me about the basket, I won't be able to tell him it came from us."

"I figure he won't mention it, other than as a passing remark or something. All I'm asking is that you don't offer to clarify the gift unless he directly puts the question to you."

"That I can do."

"I noticed that even Stover was looking a mite thin."

"Stover is a proud man. He won't ask for help, and he refused to borrow against his place. Link is extending credit, but only if a man puts up his deed to cover the debt. If we have another bad year, Link or the mayor will end up owning most of Eden."

"How are the prices at Link's store?"

"They're within reason, but no one has any money left. All of us put our money into our own shipment of goods."

"Real strange, having your wagons hit like that. If I was a suspicious sort, I might think Link had the most to gain from the robbery."

"No chance of him being in on it. He was in Denver at the time. That's where he gets all of his supplies. Mayor Harker got a wire from him the very day Andy Brown was killed. The man couldn't have been in two places at one time."

"And both the mayor and Keno were in town the whole week?"

"Harker was here. He usually attends our Sunday meetings and sings praise to the Lord at our sides. The man is trying to run his business as best he can. I don't fault him

125

for that. As for Keno, I'm pretty sure he was here the entire time, too."

"That leaves no suspects from Eden."

"I can't believe anyone from Eden would be involved in the robbery of our supplies and the murder of Andy Brown."

"You are a special sort of man, Max. You don't think anyone is capable of murder."

"If Keno Dean were reaping the rewards of running people out of the valley, I might disagree with you. He was with Quantrill at Lawrence. He's always tipping a bottle and he strikes me as a man who is lacking a soul."

"He's a cold fish all right."

"The question is, what are we going to do? The situation is desperate, Jerrod. There are people starving here in Eden. In fact, I've been in contact with others from nearby towns. There are people freezing and dying of famine all across Kansas. Those hoppers stripped the state bare. Animals have died by the thousands, crops were devastated, and the people are suffering greatly."

"I've seen a little of that myself."

"What are you going to do about it?"

"Me?"

"Other than a short ride now and again, I am not an able traveler. Besides that, Doreen has been feeling poorly these past few weeks. I would not dare leave her for any length of time."

"What are you getting at?"

"A number of people are going to die in Eden unless some kind of relief effort is mounted. I received a newsletter from back East that mentioned aid was being considered to help the farmers. One good man might be able to influence the right people and get us some help."

Jerrod frowned. "You want me to go visit the governor?"

"Mayor Harker would be the obvious choice, but he can't leave his business unattended."

"I ain't got the manners to mingle with those top-hat sorts. I'm a cow-tending ranch hand."

"You were promoted to lieutenant in the war, at what— eighteen?"

"That's different. I had some savvy about fighting."

"And this is a fight as well, Jerrod. We're fighting for our lives."

"Why me?" he asked. "There have to be a number of men in Eden who are better suited for a rescue mission."

"You were with the Union forces. Governor Osborn thinks highly of the men who served during the war. It might be the edge that helps get you in to see him."

"It's three hundred miles to Topeka."

"He who suffers for the sake of his fellow man shall be honored among the angels."

Jerrod grunted at the prophetic way Max delivered the statement. "The trouble with a promise like that is the waiting to become an angel."

"It might also garner you an ally in your quest to win the hand of Marian Gates."

"Marian?"

"Am I blind?" Max asked with a smile. "You knew whose basket you were buying at our benefit last August. I believe you and Marian would be a fine pair."

"Except for Stover hating my guts."

"Even the strongest tree bends to the wind, Jerrod. Good deeds are not all rewarded in heaven. I have a measure of influence here in Eden. While I can't change Stover's thinking, I know something that might persuade him to look at the subject from a different point of view."

"He said he would die before he would allow me to court Marian."

"Do you really believe that he thought your gift of food today was from me and my wife?"

"He seemed to accept it."

"Apple pie, you said." Max smiled. "Even at Harper's

store, there hasn't been an apple to be had for several weeks. He certainly knows where the basket came from."

"So?"

"If he can slacken his dislike for you Danmyers for the sake of his family, might he not also weaken his stance against you seeing his daughter?"

"You tell me."

"I believe I know a way to sway Stover's hatred. First, however, I need help with this relief effort, Jerrod. I can't make the journey myself. I need a strong, intelligent man to represent us. You are the man for the job."

Jerrod exhaled a deep breath. "All right, Max. I'll take a train ride and see what I can stir up."

As Tommy finished putting the army saddles on the plow horses, Marian rolled up the four gunnysacks. She secured them with a piece of rope, ducking her head against a gust of hard-granule snow.

"Wind is blowing pretty good again today." Tommy spoke the obvious. "What do you say we ride over to the Browns' old place instead of crossing the creek onto Danmyer range."

"We know there are chips over on the Danmyer pasture."

"Yeah, but Stover won't give us a whipping for going onto the Brown place. After all, it's been sold to some stranger back east. It ain't like we're stealing anything that anyone would want."

"I don't know."

"We could also warm up in the empty house before coming back."

"Now you're making sense." She shrugged. "Who knows? If Toby left in a hurry, he might have even left some food behind."

"Even if he didn't, we've got our jar of beans for lunch. We could add some snow and heat it into a broth."

"Lead the way, Tom," Marian said. "I'm with you."

The wind bit though their clothes, and the snow swirled up to pelt them in the face. The positive side of the journey was that the Brown place was closer by a half mile than the Danmyer meadow. Also, the direction of the wind meant that it would be at their backs on their return trip.

An hour put them into the Brown yard. Marian reined over to the hitching post in front of the house and stopped.

"Let's see if we can find enough to start a fire, before we start picking up chips. That way, it'll be warm for our lunch."

"Good thinking, sis," Tommy agreed.

The door opened easily, but the interior was like walking into an icehouse. Fortunately for them, Toby had left enough wood and chips to start a fire in the combination cook- and heating stove. Once the fuel was burning, they took a quick inventory of the sod house.

"Boy, he left a lot behind," Tommy said. "Look at the cupboard—it's full of pans."

"Here!" Marian was ecstatic. "He also left behind several pieces of jerky!"

"All right!" Tommy joined in happily. "I knew this was a good idea!"

They were placing the jerky next to the fire to thaw when Marian frowned and pointed. "Hey! Look at that, Tom!"

He glanced in the direction indicated and then put a questioning look on her. "Toby left behind his .50-caliber Springfield Carbine? I can't believe that. He was always bragging about his hunting."

Marian went to the bedroom and took a quick inventory. "He left behind a lot of clothes."

Tommy nodded. "Straight razor, saddle soap, and his spare boots too. What do you make of it?"

"I don't like it one bit."

"Soon as we have our lunch and get feeling back into our fingers and toes, I'm for filling our sacks with chips and getting out of here."

Marian gave an affirmative nod. Something felt very odd.

# CHAPTER 12

IT HAD BEEN a long three weeks. Jerrod wore a full-length slicker over his mackinaw. He was wearing long-handles under his warmest winter clothes, an extra pair of socks to protect his feet, and a heavy scarf wrapped about his neck. A cloth was draped over his hat and wrapped about his ears. Even bundled as he was, he was numb from the cold. The bulk of the trip had required a lot of shaking hands and waiting to speak to important people. From the lowest clerk to the office of the governor, he had pounded the streets and haunted the public officials mercilessly. There had been a measure of success—at least, promises had been made.

The sun was out, glaring up from the remaining snow, but the breeze was like a slicing knife, cutting through his clothing and penetrating him to the bone. He directed Bingo with a gloved, frozen left hand; he had removed the glove on his right and pushed it inside the front of his coat for warmth.

Bowing his shoulders against a blast of wind, he experienced relief to be nearing Eden. He was returning with good news for Max Loring, for everyone in the valley. With the right choice of words, Max might let him pass the word to some of the homesteads along his route home, specifically, the Gates family.

There was a slight movement up the trail; something dark rose up from out of the white earth. Jerrod straightened abruptly, and at that instant there came a flash from a muzzle not thirty steps away. The boom of the rifle echoed in Jerrod's ears as something white-hot streaked a path between his left arm and his chest.

Bingo jumped at the sudden noise. Jerrod rolled backward out of the saddle. He landed hard on the frozen snow and sprawled into a rut. He lay motionless on his left side, summoning his mental faculties. The slight indentation in the road was not enough for concealment, but it was adequate to prevent the ambusher from taking a second shot without moving closer.

Jerrod's breath was short and rapid. His heart hammered wildly, and there was a burning sensation along his ribs. He could feel a warm, sticky dampness from blood. He had no time to wonder if he had been hit bad. Easing his right hand inside his coat, he located his Colt and removed the thong from the hammer. He kept his eyes nearly closed, peeking through slotted cracks. His ears strained for sound and picked up the crunch of someone's approaching steps.

Risking a second shot from a cautious assailant, he decided against playing possum. He put his gloved left hand over his chest and groaned, rolling his head back and forth in feigned agony. He opened his eyes a bit wider and grimaced.

"I—I'm hit hard," he rasped. "Why—why'd you shoot me?"

The man was wearing a buffalo robe that reached the tops of his knee-high boots. He was a grizzled brute, with brooding eyes glaring from under black, bushy brows. His frosted facial hair blended in with long, greasy-looking hair that hung down in icy lumps onto his shoulders.

"Be yuh Jerrod Danmyer?" he grated.

"Who are you?" Jerrod gasped, rocking enough to one side that he now had his gun free.

"Be yuh Danmyer?" the man asked again.

"Y-yes," he gasped. "Why did you—"

The man did not have other questions. He swung the rifle barrel around, bringing it about for a finishing shot.

Jerrod could not aim from under his coat. He rotated the barrel upward and fired quickly—twice, three times!

The hairy ruffian backed up a step, as the first bullet slammed into his thigh and up into his abdomen. A second missed, but the third shot tore a path up through his jaw. He was knocked off of his feet.

Jerrod worked furiously to get his gun clear. He pulled it out from under his coat and rolled onto his knees. Quivering inside from the shock of being shot from ambush, he pointed the trembling gun at the lifeless form. The caution was unnecessary; the big man was dead.

"Durn lucky shooting," he muttered. "The way my hand is shaking, I doubt I could hit you again if I tried."

It took a few minutes to gather his wits and restore a normal breathing pattern. He assessed his own injury and discovered it to be only a slight crease. No doubt, the added clothing had made him appear a larger target than he actually was. The stranger had shot for his heart but guessed wrong as to its location.

His nerves remained unsteady while he opened the big man's coat and searched for a clue to his identity. The only thing he found in his pockets was fifty dollars in gold. A bit of searching located the man's horse, which was picketed in a drainage ditch some fifty yards off the main trail. There was nothing in his saddlebags to identify him, so Jerrod loaded him onto the horse and tied his body in place.

Once back on Bingo, Jerrod had time to reflect on the event. Why had the stranger tried to kill him? It was not mistaken identity, for he had asked Jerrod his name, wanting to make certain of his kill. That made no sense. Why would someone target him? He wasn't carrying money. In fact, he had only a handful of supplies, nothing worth killing anyone over.

Robbery was not the motive. The man had fifty dollars in his pocket. That was more gold than all of the citizens of Eden could have managed if they combined every cent they had between them. So, if he dismissed the idea of robbery, what did that leave?

Leading the man's horse, he glanced back at the lifeless body. Any answers had died with the stranger. Once he reached Eden, he would have to do some investigating on his own. If someone wanted him killed, he had better figure out the reason real quick. If there was a second attempt, he might not be so lucky.

There was a lack of humor and the usual buzz of chatter at the Sunday meeting. Faces were long, eyes stared blankly from hollow sockets, and any exposed arms and legs showed the bones protruding against tightly stretched skin. Many suffered from coughing spells, and a few were weak to the point where they could hardly walk.

Brandon was still too ill to make the trip, so Wilma had stayed behind with him. It appeared the icy chill of the late-January temperature and having to travel the snow-packed, windswept miles to Eden had kept many at home.

Max Loring gave a stirring sermon about the suffering of the children of Israel. He likened their situation to those people, driven under the whip, suffering at the hands of brutal taskmasters. His advice was to stick together, to share what little they had. He promised that aid was on the way, food and supplies to help them survive until their crops were ready for harvest.

After a lackluster hymn, Mrs. Loring brought in a tray of sweet rolls and passed out a portion to each person. The generous act put some life into the children.

Marian accepted the gift with a thank-you and took a

small bite. The roll was delicious. She relished the taste of the pastry, carefully savoring each bite. It was not until she had finished the roll that she thought of Brandon. He was home, shivering with chills, too weak to walk without someone aiding him.

A sense of shame washed over her. How could she forget his suffering? She had gobbled up the sweet roll without thinking first. Her own hunger was certainly no greater than Brandon's.

For a moment, she considered asking Mrs. Loring if she could spare another roll for her ailing brother. The idea was dismissed at once, as she saw the woman had served up the last one.

She turned to Tommy, but he was licking his fingers. He had not saved so much as a crumb either.

"What?" he asked, puzzled by her expression.

"We should have saved some for Brandon."

Realization showed on his face. "I didn't think."

"Neither did I."

Tommy looked over at their father. He had moved over next to Vernon. While the two of them were speaking quietly, he was wrapping something in a cloth and putting it into his pocket.

"Stover didn't eat his roll," he said. "Bet he'll give his to Brandon."

Marian hated the rush of guilt she felt at the thought of opposing his will. "He always thinks of us first. He's lost twenty pounds and eats barely enough to keep alive. Yet he saves his roll for Brandon and Mother."

"I guess parents naturally make sacrifices for their children."

"More than that, Tom. He knew that basket on Christmas was not from Mr. Loring."

"It wasn't?"

"Tom, when is the last time you heard of the Loring family having tortillas?"

"You mean the basket was from the Danmyers!"

"Of course."

He shook his head. "I'm surprised that Stover let us keep it."

"That's exactly what I'm saying. He always thinks of the family first. How is it that he can make so many sacrifices for us and yet want me to marry Wolfgang?"

"I'll bet you're the topic of conversation right now. You see how they keep glancing over at Wolfgang?"

"He hasn't come around the past couple weeks. I've been hoping he would find himself another girl."

"No such luck, sis." He grinned. "You're the catch of the valley. He still wants you."

"What am I going to do?"

"Look on the bright side—you won't go hungry. They have enough pigs to sell or trade and keep from going broke. In a year or two, you could be *wallowing* around in a big house, *rooting* out a good life, living *high on the hog*."

Marian did not miss all of the pig-farmer innuendos. "You really know how to put my mind at rest, Tom."

Max appeared in the crowd. He was shaking hands, wishing everyone a safe journey home, and thanking them for coming. He did not neglect the young people, often passing out sugar sticks to the very small children. As his wife had prepared sweet rolls for this meeting, he had none to offer on this day. He was still adored by the young and old alike.

"Marian . . . Tom," he greeted them. "So nice of you to brave the cold to come to the meeting."

"The sweet rolls were delicious, Mr. Loring," Marian told him. "Please give our thanks to your wife."

"Some of the thanks belong to my sister, who still lives in Ohio. Knowing how hard things have been, she sent us a little money for Christmas. We were able to buy a few things from the store."

"I'll try to remember to mention her in my prayers."

"I've been in touch with someone else you are probably including in your prayers." At her curious frown, he smiled. "Jerrod sent a wire to inform me of his progress. He was at Topeka last week seeking relief for the people in Eden. He managed to speak to the governor himself. I'm certain that something is in the works for providing aid or relief for our community."

"Jerrod—I mean, Mr. Danmyer—is doing this to help us?"

"Fine young man," Max proclaimed. "He has been gone for about a month. The wire said he would be back any day."

"Stover still hates all of the Danmyers."

"I know."

"Have you ever tried to talk to him? I mean, hating is a sin, isn't it?"

"I knew Stover back when he worked at the mines in Ohio. When the chance presented itself for us to come to this place and settle, it was Stover and I who put together a wagon train. We joined up with several German families and moved here to start a new life. Neither of us wished to end up working the mines and dying of old age at thirty.

"Laura Bonnet attended our church. She had been orphaned at fourteen and lived with a maiden aunt. For three years she slaved twelve hours a day at a clothing factory and earned only pennies. Stover offered a chance at a new life, to join our wagon train.

"It's no wonder that he blames himself for Zeb being killed. After all, he coaxed Laura Bonnet to come with us on our journey to Eden. He chose her to be Zeb's future bride, but Laura had a mind of her own. When she turned to a Danmyer, it was an insult to both Zeb and your father."

"Had she made any promise to wed my uncle?"

"Not in so many words. One time, when I spoke to her about her future, she mentioned that she was not attracted to Zeb."

"Do you think it was wrong of her to refuse Zeb and marry Faron?"

"She was free to do as she wished."

"What about me? What about my father deciding whom I shall marry?"

"There's a difference, Marian. He is your father. You must honor his wishes."

"And wed a man I don't even like?" Marian could not hide her bitterness. "When do I get to make a decision about my own life?"

"A father does what is best for his daughter."

"With no regard for her feelings?"

Max grimaced. "It is always desirable that a father seek qualities in a future husband that his daughter can admire. Survival has to be considered, the ability of a man to provide for a family. I'm sure Stover is trying to do what he feels is in your best interest."

Before she could speak again, Link Peters came pushing through the crowd. He stopped next to Max and pulled on his arm.

"Keno sent me to fetch you, Mr. Loring. He asked that you come right now."

"What's the matter?"

"Jerrod Danmyer rode into town a few minutes back—he's brung in a body."

"Someone who starved or was frozen from the cold?"

"Not this time," Link replied. "Danmyer done kilt this one all by himself!"

Marian felt her heart stop. Everyone who was within hearing distance grew silent. They all waited for Max to make the next move. He did so wordlessly, hurrying to gather up his coat.

"Did you hear that?" Tommy whispered. "Jerrod killed a man!"

"Of course I heard."

"What do you think?"

"I don't know. I wish there was some way for me to go
find out what happened."

"Stover would take a belt to you."

"Why do you think I'm still standing here with you?"

Even as they listened to others around them discuss the
news, Stover came through the crowd. "Let's go," he ordered. "It's getting late."

From the grim look on his face, it went without saying
that he wanted no questions asked concerning Jerrod.

Even as Marian started for the door, she was aware of
Wolfgang hurrying out into the cold. She tucked her
hands into her coat, instantly assailed by the cold air. By
the time she and Tommy were up on the wagon seat, Wolfgang appeared. He was carrying a sack over one shoulder.

"Ah-hah, ah-hah!" he chortled. "There be here a gift to
your family from us."

He went to the back of the wagon and placed the sack
over the side. Then he stepped back and showed his
crooked teeth in a wide grin. "I be looking forward to coming for to visit you again, Miss Marian." He gave a noncha-
lant tip of his hat. "Yah, I'm sure to look forward to it."

Marian had a sinking sensation. There was a disconcert-
ing confidence in Wolfgang's manner. She flashed a worried look at Stover, but he was all business.

"See you later, son," he said cordially to Wolfgang. "Tell
Vernon thanks again."

"Ah-hah! What are friends for!"

Stover flipped the reins and started the team moving.
Marian glanced back twice in the direction of Wolfgang.
He was standing in the middle of the road both times, eagerly waving his hand back and forth. There was something very ominous in his display, as if he was suddenly
overjoyed about something.

With growing trepidation, she cast a sideways look at
Tommy. He caught her concern and matched her puzzle-
ment with a frown of his own. There could be little doubt

that Vernon and Stover had been discussing her future. Marian's inner cold far exceeded the chill of the air outside; she felt as if her heart had suddenly turned to ice.

The mayor had been at home. After hearing Jerrod's story, he sent for Keno. The sometimes sheriff had Link go fetch Max Loring. Then they took the body over to the trading post and laid the ambusher out on the floor.

Keno stoked the potbellied stove and added some fuel to heat the room. Link returned with Max a few minutes later. After everyone was in the room, Harker pointed to the corpse.

"Danmyer claims this man tried to kill him a few miles up the road," he began. "Any of you ever seen this guy before?"

Keno used the toe of his boot to roll the man's head to one side so the mayor could take a better look. "Ugly cuss," he said. "Couldn't hardly forget a puss like that."

"He's a stranger to me," Max said.

Harker held out his hand to reveal three gold pieces, two double eagles, and an eagle. "Fifty dollars in gold coin was in the man's pocket," he said. "It would appear that someone hired this fellow to kill Danmyer."

Keno pulled a flask from his pocket and took a drink. Then he looked at Jerrod curiously. "Why should anyone want you dead, Danmyer?"

"I have no idea."

"Sure you didn't step on someone's toes or cross trails with a hard case lately?"

"No."

"What about Toby?" Link asked. "You shore 'nuff give him what-fer a few months back."

Harker gave his head a negative shake. "I can't believe that of Toby."

Link was in agreement. "Besides, I bought out Toby with a bank note. He would have had to go as far as Ellis to cash the note. Then he would have had to hire someone to come all the way back here for a killing. I don't see him wasting all that time and money for being bested in a fight."

"Toby wasn't the type to hire a killer," Jerrod concurred.

"So who would want you dead?" Harker asked again.

"I don't know."

Keno took another jolt from his flask, capped it, and stuck it into his pocket. He spent a few moments examining the body, then stood back and folded his arms. "Lucky shot, getting him through the jaw. Looks as if the bullet went right up into his brain."

"He was standing right over me." Jerrod showed the holes in his slicker. "The guy didn't know I had a gun out until I began to fire."

"And he said nothing about who hired him?"

"Only asked if I was Jerrod Danmyer."

"Got a brand on his horse?"

"No markings at all. Nothing in his saddlebags either."

Keno sighed. "Well, about all I can do is ride out and have a look. Might get a direction from where this guy came from. With the wind blowing the snow around, I doubt I can follow his trail for any distance."

"I'll go with you," Link offered.

"How did he know you would be on the trail?" Harker asked. "I mean, the guy would have had to sit there for a week or two, waiting for you to come back from Topeka."

"It's a mystery to me, Mayor."

"I'll have a look for his campsite," Keno offered. "Maybe he did just that. If so, there might be a clue to his identity at the camp."

"What do we do about the body till then, Max?" Harker asked. "This is kind of a first for me."

"Me too, Lyle. I'll have a coffin brought over. We can store the body in your back room until Keno returns. If they don't find anything, about all we can do is put him in the ground as an unknown assailant."

Harker approved the idea, then gave Jerrod a close look. "How about you, son? You said the bullet creased you?"

"I'm okay. It bled a little, but it wasn't much more than a scratch."

"Want to come over and have Doreen look at it?" Max asked.

"I'll get Maria to make me a bandage when I get out to the ranch. It's not any big deal."

"We'll be heading out," Keno said. "Link, how about you ready our horses? I'll get a few things together and meet you at the livery."

"All right."

"You say the attack was on the main trail, about five miles out, Danmyer?"

"You can't miss it. Should be able to see the bloodstain right where I shot him."

"I'll get back to you on anything we find."

Keno and Link both left the room. Max followed after them, going to round up a wooden crate for the would-be killer.

The mayor placed the three gold coins on the nearest table and sat down. "About five dollars will bury this character. What do you think we ought to do with the remaining money?"

"It isn't mine."

"It should go to his surviving family, but without knowing who he is, that is impossible. Unless you have a better idea, I propose using it toward buying some food and distributing it around." He did some quick computation in his head. "I think Link has enough flour, salt, and sugar left that we could give out a small quantity of each to every family in Eden."

"Sounds good to me."

Harker appeared pleased with the idea but still had a worried frown on his face. "Who could have been behind this, Jerrod? Why would someone want you killed? And who could have known you would be returning on that road today?"

"I have no answer to those questions, Mayor."

"You had no trouble in Topeka? And before, no run-ins while you were staying in Denver?"

"No to both."

"Think, man! People don't go out in this kind of weather and lay in wait to ambush someone for the fun of it. There has to be a motive!"

"I can't think of any."

Harker finally relaxed. "Maybe someone else has been using your name. Could be this is all a mistake. Either that, or someone has it in for your family and decided to get the one Danmyer who wasn't protected out at the ranch."

"I can't help on that count. We don't have any deadly enemies that I'm aware of."

Harker reached out and patted him on the arm. "You're all right, that's what matters. If you want to head on home, I'll see to this gent and see about dividing up the supplies. As you might have noticed, the shelves in here are pretty bare. Link and I are both about broke."

"Fit right in with the rest of the people in Eden. We're all down to cutting beans in half to have enough food to get by."

"You spoke to the governor?"

"Yes. He said they are expecting relief from several groups back east. There should be a shipment of supplies here by early spring to help the farmers get through till harvest."

He smiled broadly and clapped his hands. "Excellent! Good news at last."

Jerrod pulled his coat tightly together and headed for the door. He had killed a man, and there was no reason for it—none that he could think of. It was an unsettling feeling. Especially since he had not the slightest idea why he had been the man's target. To kill in anger, or during

the war, seemed to have purpose. It was more troubling
that there was no viable motive for this man's attack.

"I'll be seeing you, Mayor."

"If Keno turns up anything, I'll send word."

A gust of cold wind hit Jerrod in the face. He needed to
feed and rest his horse for a couple hours before making
the long ride home. He would find some coffee and get
something to eat. He felt the need for something to warm
his innards. He also hoped the short pause would remove
the bad taste from his mouth. It had been ten years since
he'd fought in the war, a decade past since he had last been
forced to kill another human being. It was not a memory
he enjoyed resurrecting.

# CHAPTER 13

MARIAN RODE BACK to the farm in silence. She suffered the memory of their departure over and over in her head. Wolfgang had been as cheerful as a kid with a fistful of candy. The reason for his behavior was painfully obvious.

As the light of day faded, she waited for the ax to fall. Her mother prepared ham and cornbread for dinner. It was the first real meal they had enjoyed since Jerrod's basket delivery in December. Even Brandon, who had grown too weak to walk more than a few steps, managed to sit up to eat.

Marian should have been thankful for a decent meal, but the food had no taste. She could not rid herself of the feeling of impending doom. After the last morsel was consumed, she helped Wilma with the dishes. Had she reserved any doubt as to her future, her mother avoided eye contact, as if ashamed to look at her.

Each plate was dried mechanically, while Marian's mind raced in search of alternatives. It was coming. There was no escape. Stover had put Brandon to bed and tested the boy for fever. His concern was fatherly, but he had a set to his eyes, a fixed expression on his face. Marian had seen such a look before—each time she or one of the boys got into trouble.

Stover was the kind of man who worked himself up to dealing out punishment. He had a temper, but it was usually under control. He dished out discipline when he considered it due. The trips to the shed were never impulsive. This time, it was slightly different. He did not have anger in his eyes, only a grim determination.

**144**

"Marian." She jumped at his speaking her name. "Put on your coat and help me with the feeding of the stock."

The stock consisted of a half-dozen chickens, two nearly starved plow horses, and a dry milk cow. It took about five minutes to feed them all. Providing water was the real chore, but they had filled the trough early that morning.

Without delay, Marian donned her coat. Tommy stood up, as if he would offer to join them, but she saw his courage fade. There was nothing he could do. Stover was the head of the family. It would be several more years before Tommy could oppose his will.

The air was still; the darkness clung over the land. It was like being surrounded by great black drapes that hung from a dark ceiling to rest against the valley floor. The moon had not yet appeared. It was neither the evening nor the cold air that made Marian shiver. She knew what was coming.

"I spoke to Vernon today," Stover began. "We agreed that you and Wolfgang should be engaged."

There it was. The words stung her like a firm hand striking her across the face. She winced and doubled her fists. "What if I don't want to be Wolfgang's wife?"

"The choice has been made for you, Marian." His voice was rigid. "I done give my word."

Marian took a step back. Stover was a domineering man, whom she had always respected and obeyed. It made it extremely difficult to oppose his will. However, this was her future, her very life.

"I'm sorry, sir, but I don't intend to have Wolfgang for my husband."

Stover's face worked. His gaze became hard and cold. "You'll do as I say, gal! I told you, I done give my word!"

With more courage than she had ever thought herself capable of, she shook her head back and forth. "You might force me to stand with him before an altar, but I will refuse my vows. I am not going to marry Wolfgang."

Stover's eyes grew wide. He had always ruled with an iron hand. It was incomprehensible that Marian would defy him. Slowly, the shock turned into seething rage. He snarled his next words.

"Listen to me, you selfish brat! This union is not only for you, it is necessary to save our farm! Brandon is too weak to get out of bed. Your mother and Tommy are both as thin as cornstalks. You, yourself, have probably lost ten pounds. We're nothing more than skeletons! Do you want everyone in the family to die from starvation?"

"Of course not."

"Well, the Krugers are our only hope to stick this through. I spoke to Harker, but he is about broke. I can't even borrow against our place unless I go to Link, and he is demanding to hold anyone's deed for the few measly supplies he provides from his store." Stover was reasoning with her, trying to force her to understand. It was strange to hear the unusual plea in his voice. "You can't think only of yourself."

Marian was besieged with guilt. Tears filled her eyes and shame flooded through her. "Please, sir," she murmured, "it isn't fair to put the survival of the family on my shoulders."

"It *is* on your shoulders, gal!" Stover announced. "You've got to do what is best for all of us."

Her brain envisioned Wolfgang. She remembered his attempt to win her over with their one kiss. It had been like pressing her lips to the mouth of a freshly caught fish. His absurd laugh echoed in her ears. It was more than she could ever accept.

"I'll go out and find a job, I'll beg on the streets of Denver, I'll dance in a saloon if I have to—but I can't marry Wolfgang! I just can't!"

"You will do as I say!"

"No! I won't!"

Stover was through talking. She could see it in the dead

set of his eyes and his clenched teeth. The muscles twitched in his jaw. "I had thought you grown up, too mature and womanlike to take to the shed again," he threatened. "Guess I was wrong."

Marian had always accepted her father's discipline. She had never refused to obey him, not even the last time when she knew the punishment was not deserved. It surprised her, almost as much as Stover, when she backed away from him.

"No, sir," she said adamantly. "I am not going to the shed. I will never go to the shed again."

Stover's bass voice boomed. "Don't make this harder than it already is, gal. Get yourself to the shed!"

Marian spun about and darted out into the yard. Stover was too surprised to grab her. She lifted her skirt and ran away from the house.

"Stop!" he bellowed. "Marian! You come back here right this minute!"

But Marian had her legs pumping. She raced into the night, trying to put enough darkness between herself and Stover that he could not keep track of her. The stupidity of her action was lost to the panic of the moment. Her only thought was to escape. She vowed to die before she ever let Stover use the strap on her again.

Jerrod had not expected to return so late. Max Loring had shared coffee with him, and the two had ended up talking until Doreen had supper prepared. She had added an extra plate, so he had sat down to a meal with them. By the time he got away, it was dark. Being so late, and knowing the hostile reception he would get at the Gates house, he took the direct route toward home.

A short way after crossing Raccoon Creek, Bingo perked her ears and alerted Jerrod. He slowed the horse immediately and pulled off his right-hand glove. Searching the darkness, he stuck his hand under his coat to rest on his

Colt. After one attempt on his life, he was not going to be caught off guard.

The black of night surrounded him except for the whiteness of the thin crust of snow that outlined the trail. There were the shadows of a few stands of scrub oak and an occasional sagebrush. Among those obscure shapes, he spied another dark form. He pulled back on the reins. It looked to be a body!

Jerrod's heart raced. His nerves were strung as tightly as the strings on a guitar. He scanned the area and strained his ears for sound, wary of some kind of trick. Seeing and hearing nothing, he stepped down from Bingo and moved over to the dusky mound. He used the toe of his boot to prod the ragged form, jabbing the lifeless body in the ribs.

"Hey! You okay?"

There came a soft moan and the outline of a face appeared from under the shaggy wrap. A shock scorched through Jerrod, as if he had been struck by a bolt of lightning! "Marian!" he gasped, dropping to his knees at her side.

"J-Jerrod!" she whispered hoarsely. "I . . . I ran . . ."

He dug her cold hands out from under the coat. "What are you doing out here?" he demanded. "Are you crazy?"

"I was . . ." A shiver cut off her words.

"Good Lord! Your clothes are wet!"

"I—I waded the creek."

"How long have you been lying here?"

"I don't know. A few minutes. I couldn't run any longer . . . I was so cold . . . I stopped to catch my breath."

Jerrod hurried to remove her damp shoes. Her feet were two lumps of ice. He feared it would only be moments before the toes would be frozen. Unbuttoning his coat, he sat down in the snow and tucked her feet to either side, against his ribs, using the warmth of his own body to thaw them.

"Lucky it's not as cold tonight. If it was down below zero, you would already be frozen to death."

"I—I know," she murmured. "I'm sorry."

He removed his other glove and pressed the palms of his hands to her cheeks, ears, and nose. She was cold, but there didn't seem to be any frostbite.

"Put your hands inside your coat and warm them in your armpits," he instructed. "Can you feel your fingers?"

"Yes" was her soft reply as she did what she was told. "It's my feet that are numb."

After a moment, he took one of her feet and used his hands to gently knead the flesh. After working on it for two or three minutes, he did the same for the other one.

"It must be working," she said through clenched teeth. "I think my feet are about to explode."

"That's the blood beginning to circulate. I did this sort of thing during the war. It's what we call a buddy system for keeping your feet from freezing. Each man rubs the other person's feet and both end up with all their toes intact."

"Do you need me to rub your feet?"

The ire returned to his voice. "I'm not the one who waded the creek. What are you doing here?"

"I ran away from home."

"Why did you run away?"

"I'd rather not say."

"I imagine Stover is out looking for you?"

"Probably."

Jerrod did some quick thinking. "We're a lot closer to my place than your house. I'll take you home with me. Then we'll sort this out."

"I don't want to be any trouble."

He chuckled at that. "Keep your feet dry while I get my blanket. We've got to bundle you up for the ride."

Bingo was a durable horse. She packed double and had them both at the ranch within an hour's time. Jake got up when he heard them come into the house. He woke Vince and Maria at once. Maria prepared some hot broth for

Marian and then whisked her away for a hot bath and a warm bed—Jerrod's bed.

Jake, Vince, and Jerrod remained in the kitchen to discuss their options.

"We have to get word to Stover," Jake said.

Vince was in agreement. "He'll be worried to death."

"I'll ride back that way," Jerrod said, "and see if I can find him."

"No, son. No need tossing fuel into the fire. Paco and Reuben can go. Stover don't have a bone to pick with those two."

Vince rose up from the table. "I'll roust them out of the bunkhouse." He plucked his coat and hat from the nearby rack and was quickly out the door.

Jake grunted. "Been a strange year, ain't it? Them Rocky Mountain Grasshoppers devastate the plains, the farmers is all starving, Andy Brown is robbed and killed by an unknown assailant, and now you find a woman frozen in the snow. Makes a man want to ride off into the hills and become a hermit."

"There is more too, Pa." Jerrod opened his shirt to reveal the ugly bluish-red line under his left arm. "I was ambushed on the way back to Eden."

"What?" He jumped up. "You've been shot!"

Jerrod waved a hand to dismiss his concern. "It's only a scratch, but it sure could have been the end of me. The guy had me lying on the ground, standing over me with his rifle pointed at my head. He could have easily killed me, but he stopped to make certain that I was Jerrod Danmyer."

Jake's brows gathered in a scowl. "You mean the fellow asked your name?"

"He was concerned that he was killing the right man."

"How do you think this character knew when you would be coming into Eden?"

"I don't know."

"How'd you get away? Did you tell him you were someone else?"

"I killed him."

Jake sat back. "You killed him? Who sent him? Did you find out anything?"

"Nothing. I took his body into town, but no one recognized him. He had fifty dollars in gold on him, that was all."

"What the deuce is going on? Why would anyone want to kill you?"

"Got me there."

Maria entered the room at the last words. "Someone wants to kill Jerry?"

Jake gestured with one hand. "Check out the nasty wound on his ribs, Maria. We about lost him."

She hurried around to peer at the injury. "Goodness, Jerry! Why didn't you say something? I'll heat some water and get something to bandage that."

"It isn't bad," he said, dismissing her concern. "How's our guest?"

"There was no skin discoloration from the cold. She was lucky that you found her before frostbite could set in. The hot broth, a soothing bath, and the comfort of your bed— she's probably asleep already."

"I can't believe she waded the creek. It's a wonder she didn't turn into an icicle."

"Why was she out there this time of night?" Maria asked.

"She said that Stover was going to beat her with a strap. She ran."

"Why was Stover going to beat her?"

"She wouldn't tell me."

"Bet the old boy is having second thoughts now," Jake said. "He must be worried sick."

"Come tomorrow, I'm going to speak to Stover," Jerrod said through clenched teeth.

"Not without some company, son. I don't want you killing him."

"Can you imagine, taking a strap to a woman her age?"

"She does seem a little grown up for such treatment."

Maria brought a pan of warm water and a strip of cloth. She had a gentle touch, but Jerrod still sucked in his breath at each application of the wet rag. Once the wound was cleansed, she applied an ointment to prevent the cloth from sticking and took a double wrap around his chest. She tied it into place and gave an affirmative nod.

"That ought to do you for now. We can change the bandage tomorrow night."

Vince came through the door and walked over to the stove. He put his hands out to warm them before speaking.

"I helped saddle the horses for the boys." He frowned, seeing the bandage around Jerrod's chest. "What happened to you?"

"It's only a precaution," Maria quipped, "in case he gets himself a broken heart."

# CHAPTER 14

IT WAS FORTUNATE that Max Loring arrived at the Danmyer ranch early. He had not had time to finish a cup of coffee when Stover Gates came storming up to the front of the house. To prevent any misunderstanding, Max was the one to answer the door.

"Max?" Stover was surprised. "What'n tarnation are you doing here?"

"Reuben and Paco came by last night after they left your place. They seemed to think you might come here with blood in your eye."

"Where's my girl?"

Max stepped out to confront Stover. Even standing on the porch, his short frame was not on an equal plane with Stover. He was forced to look up into the man's face. However, Max had always wielded a certain authority. Stover had accepted him as a leader since they left Ohio and had always shown him the utmost respect.

"Marian about died last night, Stover," Max began. "She had crossed the creek and run herself to ground." He narrowed his gaze. "You know what happens to a body when it's freezing cold, after the person works up a sweat or gets wet? When he stops to rest, he becomes a block of ice."

"She shouldn't have run from me."

"Want to explain to me why she did, Stover?"

"It's a private matter."

Max waved his hand as if dismissing the subject. "The fact is, Jerrod found your girl huddled in a snowbank, nearly frozen to death. Another few minutes last night and

**153**

you would be asking for her lifeless body today. She came that close to dying."

Stover swallowed the information and ducked his head. "I was only trying to do what's in the girl's best interest, Max. I don't want my daughter to starve with the rest of us. You and I both know we ain't all going to make it till spring."

"That's where you're wrong!" Max declared. "Jerrod brought word that a relief effort is in the works. He has volunteered to go back east and make sure some of the supplies get to Eden."

"Andy Brown tried that, too. He only got himself killed."

Max took a step forward and put his hand on Stover's shoulder. "I can't tell you what to do about Marian. She's your daughter, not mine. But we've been friends ever since your pa died in the mines. We've shared hardships together, we've prayed together, we've buried loved ones together. I would hope that my advice means something to you."

"Of course it does."

"Then hold off on the announcement about Marian's engagement. If Jerrod can bring in the supplies, won't that prove his worth?"

"Max . . ."

"Take her happiness into account, Stover. She loves Jerrod, and he loves her."

Max did not answer. He stared at the ground and turned his head from side to side. "He's a Danmyer."

"I'm only asking you to hold off on the wedding until he has time to return."

Stover did not budge. "He's got till the first day of May. That's as long as I'm going to wait. I done give my word."

Max let the matter drop. "It would be best to let your girl rest up a day or two before having her return home. She ran a fever last night and is pretty weak. It wouldn't do to have her come down sick."

"If you say so."

"I can bring Doreen out to stay here, if you don't trust any of the Danmyer family to look after her. Doreen is feeling a little better, though she still has a bit of a cold."

"I reckon they won't hurt her."

"Thanks, Stover. I'll ask that they see her home just as soon as she is strong enough to make the trip."

The big farmer didn't speak another word. He whirled about and walked over to his plow horse. Once mounted, he headed it for home, never looking back.

Jake came out to stand at Max's side. "I appreciate your making the trip out here, Max. I believe you saved us a fight."

"No doubt about that, Jake. Stover was fixed to take you all on to get his girl back."

"You think he'll change his mind about giving her hand to Wolfgang?"

"I don't know, Jake. I really don't know."

Jerrod sat down next to the edge of his own bed. Marian's eyes fluttered momentarily, then opened dreamily. At discovering him at her bedside, a light smile formed on her lips.

"How you feeling?" he asked.

"Better," she murmured softly. "My head still feels like the biggest pumpkin in the patch, but I no longer ache all over."

He reached out and placed a cool palm on her brow. The fever had subsided. She even had a little color in her cheeks.

"I've got to leave tomorrow. I won't be able to see you for a spell."

"It seems that I have to be in dire misery for us to ever be together. Either I'm stuck up to my knees in mud or frozen in the snow."

"Yes," he said, grinning. "I've been meaning to speak to

you about the lengths you stoop to for getting my attention."

"Where are you going?"

"I'm heading to the capital. There's an effort going on to send food and supplies to the victims of the locust plague. I intend to see that some of those goods reach Eden."

"Jerrod, there's something I've been meaning to mention to someone. Tom and I went over to the Browns' place the other day to pick up chips. It was cold enough that we went into the vacant house and started a fire."

"So?"

"We found all kinds of belongings left behind. There were clothes, dishes, bedding, and even a bit of food. More than that"—she peered into his eyes to judge his reaction—"Toby's rifle was there."

Jerrod let that soak in. "Toby might have left behind clothing, even a little food, but not his rifle."

"It seemed very strange to us, too."

"I'll speak to Keno and have him look into it."

Marian reached out and placed her hand on his. He smiled at the sign of affection, but her countenance was deadly serious.

"I suppose you've guessed the reason I ran away last night?"

"A few things have crossed my mind."

"Stover has promised me to Wolfgang."

"I'm working on that."

"But . . ."

He did not let her finish, leaning over to plant a gentle kiss on her lips. When he pulled back, she flashed a smile and teased, "Do you think that makes everything better?"

"Does for me."

"What about Stover and Vernon's plan to have me wed Wolfgang?"

"I'll find a way to change that. All I have to do is locate

the relief effort, gather men, wagons, and supplies, and come back to save the lives of everyone in Eden. If I manage that, the people of Eden—and Stover as well—will have to grant me whatever I ask for."

"Sounds like something from a fairy tale."

He cocked an eyebrow. "I believe I'll ask to be either the new mayor or maybe crowned king of Eden."

She playfully socked him in the ribs. He winced and she sat up quickly.

"What is it? What's the matter?"

Jerrod pressed a hand to his injured side and waited for the searing pain to subside. He tried to shrug off his reaction.

"Good punch, kid."

Marian reached out to unbutton his shirt, but he pulled back. With his wind returned and the pain under control, he gave her a negative shake of his head.

"Don't be so impetuous, little lady. Wait until we're married for that."

She was not amused. "You've been hurt! Did you have a fight with Stover?"

"No."

"Then what?"

"It's nothing," he maintained. "A little scratch I picked up yesterday. Maria saw to it that I was all patched up."

Marian obviously did not want to let the matter drop, but she finally turned back to the problem at hand.

"What did you mean—wait until we're married?"

"What else"—he winked at her—"for getting to know one another intimately."

She blushed but was not put off. "You know that isn't what I meant. How exactly do you intend to win Stover's approval?"

"Like I told you, if I get the relief supplies back here and prevent a major famine, Stover will have to consider my request to court you. If you make it known that you love me, who is going to argue that I didn't earn your hand?"

"He won't wait much longer. Do you have enough time?"

"I'll make it—if I have to carry the wagons on my back all the way!"

She still appeared uncertain. "So what if Stover doesn't agree to this idea of yours? What if helping all of us in Eden isn't enough for him to break off my engagement to Wolfgang?"

"Max is on our side."

"Mr. Loring is here?"

"We thought it a good precaution for him to be here. Stover was worried sick about you, Marian. The man searched for you all night long. When he arrived here, Max was there to greet him. Kind of took the venom out of his bite. When I return, your father will have to listen to me."

She rested a hand on his arm. "Be careful, Jerrod."

He leaned over and kissed her. It was supposed to be only a show of affection, a simple good-bye peck on the lips. However, Marian's hand slipped up behind his neck and she held him there. The wondrous contact of her mouth pressed against his was enough to curl his toes. It filled him with energy and a renewed determination to succeed. It no longer mattered what obstacles were placed before him; he would bring back the supplies to Eden or die trying.

The afternoon sun had melted much of the snow and softened the earth's frozen crust. Keno pulled his horse to a stop and pointed to the mound of dirt with something sticking out. "Take a gander at that, Link."

"It looks like the toe of a boot!"

"Bet you a beer it's Toby Brown."

"Strange that the coyotes ain't dug up the body. Guess the ground has been frozen till now."

It took only a few minutes of shoveling to uncover the corpse. A short examination showed that Toby had been felled by a single bullet.

"Reckon Danmyer had it right, guessing that Toby had never left Eden. See there? He was shot in the back."

"Indians, you think?"

"They would have cleaned out his place and stripped his body. Besides, Indians aren't in the habit of trying to hide a victim." Keno stood straight and put his hands on his hips. "No, this was not Indians."

"Danmyer and Toby had that big fight in town. You sure he didn't do this? He might have stopped to tell you about Toby's things being left at his house so's it wouldn't throw any blame his way."

"Like him or not, Danmyer is an honorable sort, Link. Had he wanted Toby dead, he would have killed him to his face."

"Who does that leave?"

Keno stared out over the open plains. He could see the Kruger place well off to the south. The buildings of Eden were mere specks off to the east. He withdrew the flask he always kept with him and tipped it up for a short swallow of whiskey. As he tucked it away, he cast a hard look at the man next to him.

"Wasn't it you who told me that Toby had sold his place?"

"Yeah. That's what I'd heard."

He continued to study the big man. "From who?"

"You mean, who told me?"

"Yes."

"I don't recollect at the moment. Someone who stopped by the store, I think. Is it important?"

"Whoever claimed they bought his place could have also been the one who killed him."

"So could anyone who heard that Toby had sold out and would be carrying money with him. Times being what they are, a good many men would have killed for that."

Keno gave a nod of his head. "I suppose you're right. Let's get into town and pick up a wagon. I don't know about you, but I ain't packing a body over my saddle."

Link took up the reins of his horse and climbed into the saddle. Keno wondered at the beads of sweat on Link's brow. He appeared nervous.

"It occurs to me that you were out of town the day those raiders attacked the wagons and killed Andy Brown," Keno said.

"Yeah, but you remember that I had to go to Denver to arrange for my store supplies."

Keno held the reins of his horse, but he did not mount. Instead, he said, "A man might wonder about the timing on that, Link. You ride off toward Denver to get supplies, and the wagons coming in from Ellis get robbed."

"Denver is west, Ellis is east, Keno. I didn't see the wagons or Andy Brown."

"All I'm saying is, it's a funny thing, you and your supplies coming in a couple of days after the raid. With no one having any money, I wonder where you got the money for a shipment of goods."

Link's eyes dilated slightly; his expression was tense. The perspiration was more prominent on his brow. Keno had done an equal amount of the digging to uncover Toby's body and hadn't worked up much of a sweat.

"Look, Keno we've known each other for a long time. You think I would lie to your face? I didn't have nothing to do with that holdup. I sent a wire from Denver to say I was running late—ask Harker! He'll tell you!"

"Anyone could have sent a wire, Link. I've been thinking back to when you told me about Toby selling out." Keno's hand rested carelessly on the butt of his Navy Colt. "I recollect that you said Toby had told you personally about selling his place."

Link licked his suddenly dry lips. "No, that ain't right. I told you, I don't remember who I heard it from."

"My place is down to a few bottles of cheap whiskey. Harker is flat busted at his bank." He narrowed his gaze, the flintlike eyes glowing. "Now I commence to wonder how it happens that you still have your shelves packed with goods and have managed to acquire a note against nearly every deed in the valley."

"Now wait a minute, Keno!" The color raced away from Link's face. He licked his lips and shifted his eyes tensely. "You're drawing the wrong conclusions here."

"The deed on Toby's place must have been worth a little money. I recall Harker saying how the people back east were paying top dollar for land . . . maybe even in gold. You know about gold—like we found on that buffalo hunter?"

"Hold on, Keno! I don't like where this is headed."

"Another coincidence maybe, what with you doing the telegraph work at your store. How do you suppose that stranger knew when and where to ambush Danmyer? Who knew the exact day and time that Jerrod would be coming to Eden?"

"I don't know!"

Keno continued, a growing confidence in his deductions. "Danmyer said he wired Harker to let him know about the governor's decision to send supplies to Eden. Harker never got the wire, but I think you did."

"Why would it matter to me? I got nothing against Danmyer."

"Except that any relief effort would hurt your chances of grabbing up all the properties in Eden. When you call in those notes, you'll bust every family in the valley. The reselling of those farms would make you a rich man."

"You know me, Keno! We've been through the toughest of times together. You really think I would try something like this behind your back?"

"I know you all right, Link. I listened to the cries of a woman you attacked. Then I watched you set fire to her house. When she and her crippled teenage boy tried to escape the flames, I saw you shoot them both down in cold blood."

"That was war, Keno. You ain't exactly innocent of killing!"

"I'm as guilty as you, Link."

"So, what's all this about Toby? You really don't think that I would shoot him in the back."

"I think you're capable of the lowest, dirtiest kind of tricks known to man. And I'm betting you hired that buffalo hunter to kill Danmyer."

Link tried to laugh as if Keno's summation were ridiculous. It was a cover as his right hand snaked downward. He yanked his pistol free from its holster and swung it about.

The gunshot from Keno's Navy Colt cut through the stillness, shattering the world with its loud report. Both men's horses danced about, spooked at the sudden noise. Keno held tightly to the reins of his mount, his stance firm, gun extended. Link glared down at him, his face a frozen mask, a sneer on his lips. Then he sagged onto the pommel and slowly slid off of his horse.

Keno watched the man fall before he put away his gun. He walked over to stand over the dead storekeeper. He hadn't killed since he had shot a man who accused him of riding with Quantrill. The emotions were still there, a strange feeling of guilt, a lingering sadness of having to take the life of another human being. Tough and feared for his deadly accuracy with a gun, Keno had never learned to shut out his inner feelings.

"You've let good people starve and suffer for your greed, Link. I'm convinced that you were responsible for killing Andy Brown, murdering Toby, and hiring someone to kill Jerrod Danmyer." He sighed. "I reckon I'll be seeing you in hell one day."

# CHAPTER 15

LINK PETERS'S NEXT of kin were a sister and her husband. Via telegraph, they agreed on a price for his general store and sold to Mayor Harker. As there was no money in Eden, they agreed to accept a note until fall harvest. Harker hired a local widow to run the store and allowed a line of credit to every farmer in the valley. With no option but to starve, every family in Eden, with the exception of the Krugers and Danmyers, went into debt to survive.

Stover was one of the last to give in, but they had to buy enough to get them through until the crops were ripe. It was a solemn afternoon that he arrived with the wagon and enough supplies to last a few weeks.

"A good many ain't going to make it," he announced at the supper table. "The store is near wiped clean, and there still be another couple months till summer."

"What are we going to do?" Wilma asked.

Stover's face was drawn. Gaunt from not eating right, strained with worry, he showed an unusual amount of uncertainty. He lowered his head and let out a deep sigh.

"We battled a drought our second year in Eden, we weathered several bitter winters, and we survived that one month-long rainstorm that had the roof dripping mud onto our supper table and into our beds. We've managed to survive the times that one of us has been down with sunstroke or had a life-threatening cold. We come through it all"—he uttered a mild oath—"only to be beaten by a horde of locusts."

"We ain't beat yet, sir," Tommy said. "It won't be long until there are rabbits to hunt and fish in the creek. We

163

can search out wild onions or berries. If need be, I can get a job and earn some money. We'll make it."

Brandon nodded his head. Still weak, but finally recovering from his cold, he joined in with his brother. "Tom is right, sir. In another week or two, I'll be ready to help on the farm. We'll be okay."

Stover showed a rare smile. "You boys make me ashamed of feeling sorry for myself. I reckon you're right. With a decent spring and the grace of the Lord, we'll get through till the crops are up."

Marian listened quietly. She felt incredibly selfish for not also volunteering her help. However, she knew the main contribution she could offer would be to agree to marry Wolfgang. As his wife, she could provide her family with enough pork to get them through. But as much as she loved her family, it remained a distant and extreme last resort.

"Perhaps Mr. Danmyer will have some success on his mission to the state capital," Wilma suggested. "He might arrive with the donated supplies Max mentioned at the Sunday meeting."

"I'll not be in debt to a Danmyer," Stover declared.

Tommy took up with Wilma. "The stuff wouldn't be from him. It's a relief effort by the people back east. They know how badly the farms were hurt by the hoppers. A good many of them depend on our corn and grain for their own needs."

"Yeah, well, don't be counting on a Danmyer for anything, that's all I'm saying. I'd sooner trust a stepped-on rattlesnake."

Jerrod paced the foyer impatiently. Three weeks he had been traveling, talking to people, trying to get some action. There were reports of missing supplies, of corruption, of theft. But so far, all he had heard were rumors.

"The secretary will see you now, Mr. Danmyer," a young

man said, interrupting Jerrod's gloom. Jerrod quickly followed his lead into a large office. A man dressed in an expensive suit sat behind a finely polished oak desk. There were papers spread before him, piles of addressed envelopes stacked on one corner, and a list in his hand.

"Sit down, Mr. Danmyer."

Jerrod took a chair opposite the desk and waited.

"This pile of letters are but a few of the thousands of requests we have received for aid." He peered at Jerrod over a pair of spectacles. "I have also interviewed a dozen representatives from farming towns or communities. Hundreds of families have been driven from their land and thousands are starving, all due to the massive migration of those Rocky Mountain locusts last summer. We've had reports of countless deaths. Many have died from hunger and the bitter cold of winter."

"I certainly realize that Eden is not the only township that is suffering, Mr. Secretary."

"We have mounted a number of relief efforts, Mr. Danmyer. I must tell you that our success has been less than dazzling. The fact of the matter is, we are considering asking the army for help. There has been so much theft and corruption that the soldiers from Fort Hartsuff have been ordered to take charge of the distribution of emergency supplies."

"Excuse me, Mr. Secretary, but I recall hearing about the post on the north fork of the Loop River. It isn't all that big."

"They changed the name to Fort Hartsuff in December, in honor of Major General George L. Hartsuff."

"Yes, but the fort is in Nebraska. It will take them months to get as far as Eden. Especially since the garrison there is only about a hundred men."

"I'm aware of the logistics of the situation, Mr. Danmyer. That is why I have agreed to speak to you personally. You are a rancher, are you not?"

"Yes, sir."

"But you are not here for yourself? You have come to ask for aid for the farmers of Eden?"

"That's right. The town mayor has a business to run. The farmers are barely surviving. I was about the only one able to make the trip."

"We have a limited amount of supplies available," the man said. Then, eyeing Jerrod with a skeptical gaze, he continued, "However, I believe you are a man I could trust."

"Thank you, Mr. Secretary."

"Three wagons is about what we would allot to a community of that size," he said flatly. "If you can provide the wagons and the men to drive them, I will sign a requisition for enough provisions to get the people of Eden through the worst of this."

Jerrod sprang to his feet and stuck out his hand. "You've got yourself a deal, Mr. Secretary! I'll have them rounded up by tomorrow morning."

The man rose up from his chair and shook hands. "I'll see to the supplies. The warehouse is next to the train station. The man who runs it will have the necessary paperwork for you."

Jerrod left the building with a spring in his step. His efforts had paid off at last. It was a great feeling of accomplishment. With three wagons of supplies, everyone in Eden should make it through to harvest. He needed to hire a couple of good men and lease wagons and horses from a local freight company. He didn't have enough money to cover the entire bill, but he would send off a wire to Mayor Harker and have him stand good for the balance. Everything was going to turn out fine.

"This telegram arrived this morning," Mayor Harker told Keno. "Danmyer is headed this way with three full wagons of supplies. He needs me to help pay for the freight."

"Shouldn't be much," Keno guessed. "If I was on a mission to help save people's lives, I'd charge practically nothing."

Harker grinned. "You have mellowed in your old age. I remember the young Keno Dean, the most feared man in all of Kansas."

"That was a lifetime ago. I was wild and crazy back then. I never thought about the consequences of anything I did. I can tell you, I ain't proud of a good many things in my past."

"We all have our crosses to bear, Keno." He gave a cynical grunt. "That's why we came to Eden. It pains me that Link was doing us dirt behind our backs. He made a promise to stay the straight and narrow when we settled here. Hard to take, him killing Andy, robbing those supplies, then murdering Toby for their farm."

"Took me a while to figure out how he stole those supplies. The wire coming from Denver was real smart."

"I remember. He wired to say one of his wagons had to have a new axle and he was running a day or two late. I suspect he went down the line a piece and tapped into the wire. Since Link was the usual telegrapher, the guy running his store for him didn't have enough experience to know the message was not coming from Denver."

"Yep. Then he hires some goons and attacks the wagons. He hauls the stuff back to Ellis and sticks it on the train. We find the empty wagons while he is unloading the loot in Denver. He comes here with his own wagons filled with the stolen supplies. Right tricky."

"Wonder why he paid someone to try to kill Danmyer?"

"Probably afraid he would learn about his little deception in Ellis. After all, Danmyer was looking for help to provide supplies. If he talked to the wrong man, he might learn about how the delivery of goods was returned to Ellis and then shipped on to Denver."

"Either that," Harker said, "or he was trying to stave

off any relief effort. Killing Danmyer would have slowed down the word that help was coming. Without the news of aid being on the way, Link might have been able to persuade several of the farmers to give up their deeds and leave."

"Yep. That makes sense."

"How about the wire from Danmyer? Do we take any chances with this shipment?"

"What's on your mind, Harker?"

"I think you and I ought to ride out and meet those wagons—a little added security to make sure they arrive this time."

"Good thinking," Keno replied. "Need to make sure these supplies reach their destination."

"I'll see if I can find a couple more men to ride with us. What do you think? First light tomorrow?"

"I'll be ready."

Wolfgang pulled the wagon to a stop. Marian sighed, hating the ruse of the courtship. The only positive side was the basket lunch Wolfgang had brought from home. His mother was a fine cook and the Gates household had been surviving on a few scraps daily. She welcomed a real meal.

Once down from the wagon, she reached for the blanket behind the seat, prepared to spread it on a smooth place for their picnic.

"Ah-hah!" Wolfgang snorted, taking hold of her hand and pulling her aside. "I'm going to tell you a big surprise, Miss Marian. Are you ready?"

"What surprise?"

"We can begin to plan our wedding. Your father has allowed that we can be engaged. It shall be announced at next Sunday's meeting."

Marian stared at him horror-struck. "What?"

"Yah, you bet. We be the happiest two people in Eden. We build a big house and have plenty of kids."

Marian jerked her hand away from Wolfgang. "I told you that I love another man! Doesn't that bother you?"

Wolfgang shrugged off her words. "You will learn to love me. I know you will. You see. We be real happy."

Recalling how Vernon and Stover had talked for an hour after the Sunday meeting, Marian now realized they had been dealing for her body and soul. Stover had not even dared to speak to her about it. After her running away, he must have been uncertain as to how to approach her.

*Honor thy parents! Where is the honor in doing something as sneaky and underhanded as this?*

"I'm sorry, Wolfgang," she said firmly. "I cannot marry you."

The smile and confidence departed from his expression. "Listen to me, Miss Marian," he pleaded. "I make you good husband. I treat you special. I will never raise a hand or my voice to you. I will love you with my full heart."

She saw the adoration that shone in his eyes and oozed from his every word, but his feelings were not enough. She had to be able to live with herself. "You are a very nice man, Wolfgang, and I know you would make a fine husband, but the answer is no."

"You are the daughter of your father. He has spoken in this matter. We are to be wed."

Marian was torn between rage at her father and pity for the lovelorn Wolfgang. She hated to hurt him, but the false courtship was at an end. Better to set him straight, before the charade escalated any further.

"I can't help what Stover has told your father. I can't marry you. There is another man who has control of my heart."

"It be Danmyer!" He snarled the name. "You should think another time, Miss Marian. Your father will not allow you to marry him! Never!"

She spun about and strode briskly away.

"Wait! Miss Marian, wait!"

It was two miles back to her house, but Marian was walking with purpose. Even when Wolfgang came alongside in the wagon, she refused his offer to get aboard the wagon. After a half mile or so, the young man finally realized he was wasting his time. He muttered a halfhearted farewell and turned the wagon for home.

Marian glanced in his direction and her ire increased. Wolfgang's shoulders sagged and his head hung low with defeat. The rejection had wounded him deeply, and she hated being forced into hurting him. A fire burned in her blood and her temper was fully aroused at the turn of events. The exercise of walking did not slake her fury. She saw the Loring carriage in the yard, but did not slow her pace. She entered the house with purpose and slammed the door.

Stover and Wilma were at the table, along with Max and Doreen. They were engaged in a game of dominoes. Stover looked at her with surprise on his face, a knowing light shining within his eyes.

"You have given me no alternative, Stover," she snapped harshly. "I'm packing my things and leaving home. If you try and stop me, I'll run away the first time you turn your back!"

"What on earth?" Wilma asked.

Stover rose up from his chair. "Marian! Don't you use that tone of voice in this house."

Marian faced the four of them. "I'm sorry if my tone offends you or our guests. I realize that a slave should not speak to her master in such a way, but I'm through being a slave!"

Stover's face twisted menacingly, but Max reached out and quickly took hold of his wrist. Before anyone else could speak, Max was on his feet and in control of the situation.

"Why don't we discuss this problem? I'm sure that no one needs to lose their tempers." He put a quiet plea into his voice. With a tug, he forced Stover to sit down. "Perhaps you could start, Marian?" he coaxed. "Tell us what is the matter?"

Marian's throat constricted, her eyes burned with tears. "I don't wish to be a bad or ungrateful child, Mr. Loring. I've tried to be a good daughter."

"I think we would all agree with that," he encouraged gently. "So what is wrong, child?"

"Just that!" She drew a second wind. "I'm not a child! And I'm not an object of barter or a beast of burden to be sold at auction."

"Sold?"

"Stover has told Vernon that I will marry Wolfgang," she said tightly, "but I won't! I can't give away my life! I want some say in who I marry."

"You'll do as I say!" Stover bellowed.

"Wait a minute, Stover. Let her speak!" Max held up his hands to quiet them both. Then he nodded to Marian. "Please go on."

She sighed deeply. "I don't love Wolfgang. In fact, I can barely tolerate him. I would be miserable being married to him."

"Stover?" Max rotated to him.

"She's my daughter. I want her to have a good home. Wolfgang would see that none of her kids ever went hungry. He would be a good provider. He dotes on her. What more could she want from a husband?"

Max donned his fatherly expression. "There is someone else, isn't there, Marian? Jerrod?"

Marian squared her shoulders and lifted her chin. "Yes."

Stover fumed. "I won't have—"

Max pointed at Stover. "Wait!" he commanded. "Don't say another word. There is something you don't know, something Doreen and I have kept from you for a number of years. I believe the time has come to tell you the whole truth."

❧

"What truth could possibly have anything to do with my daughter and who she is to marry?"

"You hate the Danmyers. It is the reason you would never consider Jerrod as a husband for Marian, isn't that right?"

"I'd sooner see her dead."

"Because of the way Zeb died?"

"That's right."

Max lowered his head. "Doreen was at the Danmyer house when Zeb came gunning for Faron Danmyer. She . . . well." He looked at his wife. "Maybe you should tell it, dear."

Doreen was a very soft-spoken woman, but no one was more respected in all of Eden. She gathered her thoughts and, to avoid Stover's hard glare, directed her words at Wilma.

"Max had gone off hunting with Jake Danmyer. I was in the house with Laura and Faron when Zeb arrived. He had obviously been drinking, as he was using foul language. I was at the window when Laura and Faron went out to speak to him. Zeb called Laura a filthy name and drew his gun. He shot Laura and turned the gun on Faron. He missed Faron, who fired back several times. One of his bullets hit Zeb and killed him instantly."

Wilma was frowning. "Did you say that Zeb shot Laura?"

"I treated and dressed her wound. The bullet grazed two of her ribs. It bled quite a bit, but it wasn't life threatening."

"No one said anything about Zeb shooting Laura," Stover put in. "Why wasn't I told?"

Max let out a deep breath. "Faron and Laura both felt badly about what had happened. After all, Laura had come to Eden with the expectation of marrying Zeb. She didn't intend to fall in love with Faron, it simply happened. They didn't want Zeb to be remembered for having tried to kill a woman. Faron said to not say anything about how

Zeb died, only that the two of them had been in a gunfight. It was their intention to save you additional pain."

"My pain?" Stover was aghast.

"You've blamed the Danmyers all these years," Doreen said to Stover, "thinking the worst of them. I know you've cursed them, treated them like dirt, and turned a number of other folks against them."

"Yes," Max joined in with Doreen, "and they have accepted the condemnation without complaint. Faron and Laura felt a lot of guilt over your brother's death. No matter how he died, Zeb was not a bad man until he got drunk and tried to kill them both. They wished to spare his memory."

There was a long silence around the table.

"I should have been told," Stover said at length. "I—" He sagged back against his chair. "I can't believe Zeb would actually try to kill Laura. I thought he loved her."

"The liquor worked on his anger and humiliation," Max suggested. "He was out of his head."

Stover set his jaw. "But to try to kill a woman? What kind of man would do that?"

"How sad," Wilma murmured, "that we have wrongly shown contempt to the Danmyers all this time. I feel very ashamed."

"You should have put us straight years ago, Max," Stover said.

"I felt obliged to honor the wishes of Faron and Laura. There was no reason not to until this courtship between Marian and Jerrod."

"Courtship!" Stover growled. "I've been against that man every step of the way. How can there be any courtship?"

"I am in love with him," Marian spoke up.

Wilma looked into her eyes. "Are you certain that you haven't been seeking his company only to spite your father?"

"No, Mother. I love him because of the way he makes me feel—like I'm the most special person on earth."

The room was silent until Stover finally cleared his throat. All eyes turned to him.

"It won't be necessary for you to leave home, Marian. I'll ride over and speak to Vernon. I'll take the blame for offering the engagement to Wolfgang. You don't have to marry him."

# CHAPTER 16

JERROD AND THE two men he had hired drove the three wagons toward Eden, Jerrod in the lead. When they were a few miles from town four men on horseback approached. Jerrod recognized Keno Dean and Mayor Harker, but he did not know the other two.

He drew back the reins to stop the wagon procession and waited for the men to arrive. A smile was on Harker's face.

"You made it, my boy! That's great!"

Keno grinned, too. "Looks like a lot of people are going to be mighty glad to see you, Danmyer. I never figured you'd manage it."

"It took some convincing," Jerrod replied. "Managed to get the wagons on loan, but I didn't have enough money to cover everything. I expect you'll stand good for the balance, Mayor?"

"Certainly," Harker said, still showing a wide smile. "I'll be glad to contribute to such a worthy cause." He reached into his pocket. "In fact, I've got the payment right here."

Jerrod's smile froze on his face. What Harker pulled from his jacket was a small pistol. Before Jerrod could shout a warning, Harker aimed at Keno's back and pulled the trigger.

The other two men were moving at once, both with their guns drawn. Jerrod grabbed for his rifle, but a bullet slammed into his shoulder and knocked him off the wagon seat. He tumbled to the ground and sprawled into the dust.

Gunshots rang in his ears. Jerrod knew his two hired men had no chance. Rolling on his side, he attempted to get his Colt, but a shadow fell over him. Harker was there, gun in hand, ready to finish him off.

"You are one tenacious man, Danmyer. I sent that buffalo hunter to kill you last time. I can't believe he failed. The man said he could hit a target from a thousand yards."

"What's the deal, Harker?"

"The deal?" He laughed. "You don't even know about Link, do you?"

"Link?"

"Keno killed him the day after you left town. He discovered that Link had killed Toby Brown." He grunted his contempt. "Can you imagine Keno thinking that Link had the brains to mastermind a deal of this size?"

"What kind of deal?"

"I told you last summer, Danmyer. There are buyers back east ready to pay top money for farmland, especially developed land with water. With the locusts destroying all of the crops, I can have it all. With the exception of your place and the Krugers', everyone in Eden has signed their deeds over to me for loans. Link did the legwork, but I always had the capital. It was all my idea from the start."

"You two-faced vermin."

The other two men rode back and dismounted next to Jerrod. They walked over to stand at Harker's side.

One of them spoke up. "The two drivers are done for."

"That only leaves you, Danmyer. Any last words?"

Jerrod had his hand on his gun, but three muzzles were pointing at his head. He had no chance, none whatsoever.

"You might tell Marian Gates that I love her," he said quietly. "And as for you, Harker—rot in hell!"

The mayor snickered. He cocked the gun in his hand and aimed right at Jerrod's face. "Be seeing you there, Danmyer."

A gun blast filled the air—a second—a third!

Jerrod flinched, knowing he had lived his last moment.

But to his shock, the two hired gunmen went down instead. Harker sagged to his knees and teetered for a moment, a look of total disbelief on his face. Then he pitched forward and lay still.

Keno was up on one knee, his left hand pressed against a crimson stain on his chest. He lowered his gun and attempted to sit down. The effort put him onto his back.

Jerrod crawled over to him. A quick inspection showed that Keno had only a few moments of life in his body. Jerrod lifted the man's head onto his lap.

"You saved my life, Keno."

The gunman closed his eyes, as if gathering the strength to speak. "You knew I rode with Quantrill, but no one ever pointed a finger at Harker or Link. We were all together at Lawrence, Kansas. Harker robbed the stores and a bank. Link raped and murdered a woman—killed her crippled boy, too. Me . . ." He coughed. "I helped to shoot down a bunch of green recruits. They were mostly kids, just enlisted to go off and fight. They weren't even armed."

"We all did things during the war that we aren't proud of, Keno," Jerrod said, trying to ease the man's death.

"We split up from Quantrill, once the army closed in on him. We used the money Harker had stolen to start our own places in Eden. We took an oath to live our lives like decent men." He grunted. It caused him to cough a second time, doubling over from the pain. "I should have known Link didn't have the brains for swindling everyone out of their deeds. Harker acted so reformed . . . he really had me fooled."

"Easy now, Keno. I'll get you and the wagons to Eden. You'll make it."

"You don't lie worth a damn, Danmyer. I'm dead and"—he closed his eyes tightly from another jolt of pain—"and headed for hell."

Jerrod could do nothing. Keno stiffened. A long sigh escaped his lips as the breath of life left his body. Jerrod lowered him gently and glanced at the three men Keno had killed with a single shot each.

"Maybe you won't go to hell after all," he said aloud. "Not if I can manage to get these supplies to Eden."

As soon as word reached the Gates family that the mayor and Keno had ridden out to meet the incoming supply wagons, Marian had gone into Eden to wait. There was little to do—the bank, store, and tavern were all closed. She spent most of her time with Doreen Loring, waiting and watching. When, at last, she saw a tendril of dust, she hurried down the main road to meet the wagons.

At first, she was satisfied to walk at a quick pace. However, when she saw that there were no riders on horseback accompanying the wagons, she hurried even more. *What had happened to the mayor and Keno?*

Drawing closer, she could see only one man atop the first wagon. The other wagons had no drivers. The teams were attached with a lead rope to the wagon ahead, and four horses were trailing along to the rear of the last wagon. Marian began to run.

Jerrod could hardly focus. A red haze covered the world and distorted his vision. He thought someone was coming toward his unusual wagon train, but he could not be certain. The combination of no sleep and suffering from having a bullet pass through his shoulder was causing him to see a good many things that were not so.

"Jerrod!" he heard a distant voice cry. "Jerrod! Are you all right?"

He shook his head. "Can't be Marian," he mumbled. "How would she get out here in the middle of nowhere?"

She managed to maneuver around the rolling wheel and climb up alongside him. He felt her next to him, but still did not believe she was actually there.

"Jerrod!" Marian cried. "Speak to me! Wake up!"

"Dag'gum, it is you!"

Her arms flew about his neck. "Jerrod! What happened?"

With a great deal of effort, he shook the fog from his brain. "Keno saved me from ambush." He paused. "Couldn't save the two guys I had hired to help haul the supplies."

"You mean Mayor Harker tried to kill you?"

He explained the chain of events, growing more lucid with each passing moment. When he finished, he looked into her shining eyes. "What about you? How did you get out here?"

"It's only a short way to town. I saw the dust of the wagons."

"Yeah, but . . ."

"And Stover has allowed that you can come courting."

"He did?"

"And . . ."—she leaned over and kissed him—"you had better come often."

"I don't understand. What happened? Why the change of heart?"

"Let's say that, from this point on—as soon as we get you on the mend—things will be a whole lot different."

"That so?"

"Yes."

Jerrod managed a tight grin. "Say, mud kitten, did I ever get around to telling you that I love you?"

"Not in so many words."

Jerrod leaned over and kissed her again. "Well, I do."

She smiled. "Remember those last two words. You'll need them soon enough."